A *Summer* TO REMEMBER

SHANELL KEYS

Copyright © 2024 Shanell Keys.

All rights reserved. No part of this book may be reproduced, stored, or transmitted by any means—whether auditory, graphic, mechanical, or electronic—without written permission of both publisher and author, except in the case of brief excerpts used in critical articles and reviews. Unauthorized reproduction of any part of this work is illegal and is punishable by law.

ISBN: 979-8-89419-028-0 (sc)
ISBN: 979-8-89419-029-7 (hc)
ISBN: 979-8-89419-030-3 (e)

Because of the dynamic nature of the Internet, any web addresses or links contained in this book may have changed since publication and may no longer be valid. The views expressed in this work are solely those of the author and do not necessarily reflect the views of the publisher, and the publisher hereby disclaims any responsibility for them.

One Galleria Blvd., Suite 1900, Metairie, LA 70001
(504) 702-6708

CHAPTER 1

It is hard for anyone to find love these days, especially if you're born different, like me. I have always been a romantic, always dreamed of meeting my prince charming someday and having him ride in on a white horse and save me. I don't know what he would be saving me from, but he would be there to save me if I ever needed saving. After all, that was how it was in all the fairy tales my mom used to read to me when I was a little girl. Sleeping Beauty, Cinderella and Snow White all had one thing in common, a happy ending or as they call it 'happily ever after.' But the reality tends to be quite different. There is no white horse, no prince charming, and definitely no happily ever after. I was pondering this one day when my cell phone began to buzz in my pocket. I knew who it was before I even looked at the screen.

"Hi, mom." I said with a sigh. I continued to load some dishes into the dishwasher with my free hand.

"Hey Sammy, I'm so glad I caught you at a good time. Do you have a minute to talk?"

My mother's voice was quiet, almost a whisper. I rolled my eyes at the fact that she still used my nickname even though I had asked her not to hundreds of times. I preferred my full name, Samantha. Besides, no one except her had called me Sammy since I was a child.

"Sure mom, what's up?" I asked, guessing what it was before the words came out of her mouth.

"It's your brother." She said, with a tone of worry and desperation in her voice.

She was referring to my younger brother, Freddy. At the ripe old age of fifteen, he had been giving my parents all sorts of trouble recently. Skipping school, hanging out with the wrong crowd, and he had even been caught vandalizing an abandoned house with a group of kids, which resulted in six months of community service. We had all tried to get through to him, to make him realize these bad choices could have some serious consequences, but nothing seemed to work. In his mind, he was right, and we were all wrong.

"What did he do now?" I asked, not trying to hide the annoyance in my voice.

"Well, it's nothing new, just the same old thing, and to be honest with you, your father and I don't know what to do anymore. His grades are just awful, even though I know he's smart. He skips school all the time, and he hangs out with these hoodlums that are always up to no good. And, the attitude, the disrespect is just appalling. I never remember you giving us this much trouble when you were his age. You were always so easy."

I snorted, trying to hold back my laughter. "I was hardly easy, mom. I was just challenging in different ways. I think it's just been so long you forgot."

She paused while she thought about what I said. "Well, at least you respected me and your father. Freddy just doesn't seem to care."

"I'm sorry he's giving you so much grief." I said. "But what do you want me to do about it? He hardly respects me any more than he does you or dad. I can try to talk to him, but I'm not sure that will help."

"Well, actually, I was hoping he could come stay with you for the summer?"

I was quiet for a moment, trying to process what she was saying to me. "You want Freddy to stay with me all summer?"

"Yes. Your father and I have talked it over and we really think it's the best thing to do. We've been trying to plan this trip to Paris forever, and we honestly just need a break. Besides, maybe this is the sibling bonding time you and Freddy need. What do you think? You don't need to decide today, but can you at least think it over?"

The silence was defining as I thought about how I should respond to my mother's request. Would I be a jerk if I just said no? And would this really be the sibling bonding time she hoped for, or would we both end up fighting the whole time? I felt like there was no good answer, but in the end, I just said;

"Ok, I think that can work."

I could hear my mother's relief on the other end.

"Really?"

"Yes, really."

"Ok, well his last day of school is the 7th of June, so we can drop him off on the 8th. And Sammy, I can't thank you enough for this."

I sighed, wondering what the hell I'd just got myself into. "You're welcome, Mom."

I started cleaning out my guest room that afternoon, and I realized what a mess it was. Nobody had stayed in it for as long as I could remember, so it had become my catch all room, the junk room. As I cleared out some old photos from one of the nightstand drawers, I started to reminisce. One of the pictures was of mom and dad with the two of us on the beach in Santa Cruz, all with big smiles on our faces. That's when Freddy was going through his awkward toothless phase, and I had to laugh at the big gap where his two front teeth used to be. He was excited though, because that meant he was going to grow his big adult teeth, and he thought that was what was going to make him a man. Little did we know that the sweet little boy in that picture with the mop of curly dark blond hair would become the unruly teenager he was today. I was disappointed when my parents told me I was going to have a brother. I had always dreamed of having a sister. Someone who I could play dolls with and paint my nails with. Someone who I could gossip about girl stuff with. But as soon as I saw him, I was in love. I was nearly eight when he was born, so I was old enough to help with bottles and diapers and things like that. I quickly became like a second mom to him; I would even sing to him every night.

I love you in the morning,
And in the afternoon
I love you in the evening,
And underneath the moon
Skidda marink a dink a dink
Skidda Marink a do
I love you.

When I would sing that song to him, he would smile and fall asleep in my arms. It was the best feeling ever, and it made me realize I wanted to be a mom someday. But right now, I just wondered how I was going to survive the summer with a rebellious teenager in the house.

CHAPTER 2

The last day of school in my First-grade classroom at Crocker elementary was bittersweet. It was only my second year of teaching, and I absolutely loved what I did. Many of my students brought gifts. Flowers, candy, cards, and Knick knacks that said 'world's greatest teacher' covered my desk, and I couldn't help but smile as I looked down at my students, who all seemed to have grown so much since I first met them in the fall.

"Boys and girls, you have all been wonderful students this year. I think you are all more than ready for second grade. I want you to remember everything you have learned this year and keep writing in your journals over the summer. And don't forget to read the books I gave you." I picked books for each of them based on their interests, so I knew they would be excited to read them. One of my students, a red-haired boy named Charles raised his hand. "Yes, Charles?" I asked, pointing to him.

"Are we ever going to see you again?" he asked, sadly.

I smiled. "I am sure I will see some of you at recess time, and you are always welcome to come by and say hi. I would love to see how you are all doing, so you are welcome to come see me anytime."

Bonnie raised her hand next, a cute little girl with dark hair and freckles across her nose. "But I will be moving this summer, so I won't be coming to this school anymore." She said with tears in her eyes.

"Well, I am sure we can keep in touch by E mail." I said sympathetically. "We are lucky to have technology that helps us keep in touch no matter where we are. And I am sure you will do great in your new school."

She nodded, but I noticed she still looked sad. "It won't be the same, Miss Goodwin. All my friends are here, and you're the best teacher ever. I don't want to go to second grade. Can't you just keep us all in first grade?"

"Yeah, we want to stay with you." Another student shouted from the back.

"It doesn't work that way." I said, suddenly feeling a little misty-eyed myself. "I will miss you all, but like I said, you are all ready for second grade. I wouldn't be doing you any favors if I held you back in first grade. It's like the story we read about the baby bird who was learning to fly. You all have strong wings, and you are ready to fly wherever life takes you. That might be a different classroom or even a new school, but you are all going to do great. Now it's almost time for the bell to ring, so I want you all to get your back packs and line up."

They all quietly retrieved their back packs and lined up. Several of them stopped to give me a hug on the way, and I was reminded of how much I would miss each of their darling faces.

After all of my students had gone home, I finished cleaning out my classroom. I brought a wagon to carry all of the gifts and items I didn't want to leave all summer. I was almost ready to leave when the principal, Mr. Hubert walked in.

"Miss Goodwin, did I catch you at a good time?" He asked, straightening his glasses.

"Sure." I said. "I was just finishing up in here."

He nodded. "Great. Well first, I wanted to thank you for another great year. You have been a great addition to our school community."

"Thank you, Mr. Hubert." I said, beaming with pride.

"I just wanted you to be aware I did receive a complaint from a parent about a certain lesson you were teaching. It seems it became a discussion about the afterlife?"

My heart stopped. I did have a discussion with my students. It happened when one of them lost a beloved grandfather to cancer and asked what happened after you die. I had only been trying to give hope and comfort, but maybe I overstepped boundaries. I talked about the wonderful afterlife that was waiting for us all, and the children had all been intrigued by this thought. But we weren't a religious school, and all the paperwork I had been given made it clear I had to teach by the curriculum given to me by the state.

"I'm sorry if I went too far with that." I said. "One of my students had a loss in his family and I was only trying to comfort him."

Mr. Hubert nodded. "I understand. Just remember this is a touchy subject for some parents. Everyone has their own beliefs. I just wanted you to know, and moving forward, you can always come to me for advice on how to deal with questions the kids might ask. Like I said, you have been a great addition to our school, and I would hate to lose you as a teacher."

I nodded, realizing this was more of a warning than anything else. I had gotten used to being called out for the way I thought, but somehow it just didn't get any easier.

My parents' car was already parked in my driveway when I arrived home that afternoon, and I realized how desperate they were to hand my brother over and hop on a plane to Paris. My dad jumped out of the driver's seat and opened his arms for a hug, which I gladly accepted. I had always been a bit of a daddy's girl. Mom stepped out of the passenger seat and waved to me with a smile.

"Hi, Dad, hi, Mom." I said, peeking through the back-seat window where Freddy sat, looking down at his phone. His dark blonde hair hung over his eyes, and he looked entranced on whatever game he was playing.

I knocked on the window. "Hey Freddy. Happy Summer break!" I started singing the Alice Cooper song '*Schools out for summer.*' My brother finally emerged from the car.

"Can we go inside? Its hot out here."

He stomped toward the door, looking down at his phone the whole time.

"Nice to see you, too." I mumbled as I retrieved my keys and let everyone in. I had put a pot roast in the crock pot for dinner, and the aroma made me realize how hungry I was. I had been so busy in my classroom I hadn't eaten much that day.

Freddy plugged his nose. "What is that smell?"

"Now Freddy, be polite." Our mother warned.

"That smell is a delicious pot roast, with potatoes and carrots." I told him.

He sighed. "Didn't mom tell you I'm a vegetarian now?"

"No, she didn't." I said, my jaw tightening with annoyance. "But like I said, there are vegetables, too."

"But they're touching the meat."

Our parents both shot him a stern look and looked at me apologetically. I just smiled, trying to break up the tension which was so thick you could cut it with a knife.

"I'm sure I can whip up a salad or something. Why don't you put your things in the guest room and get settled in?"

He rolled his eyes as he walked toward the guest room. "This summer is going to suck big time." He mumbled before he shut the door behind him.

"Isn't he just a joy right now?" My mom said sarcastically.

I laughed. "It looks like you two can use a drink. And you're welcome to stay for dinner. There's plenty for everyone. So, what will it be? Wine? Beer? Or one of my specialty cocktails?"

My mother smiled, thinking it over. "Just surprise me."

⸎

As we all sat around sipping on a glass of Pinot noir, I felt grateful to have such wonderful and caring parents. They truly had the kind of love most people dream of, and it gave me hope that it could happen for me someday. For the first six years of my life, it was just mom and me. It wasn't that my dad didn't want to be part of my life, he was kidnapped by a mad man before mom even found out she was pregnant with me. Luckily, we found him before it was too late. I think that made me appreciate him even more, and I never took a moment with him for granted. We also have one very important thing in common. We are both what you call 'mediums', meaning we can communicate with dead people.

"So how has work been, dad?" I asked, taking another sip of wine. He worked for the special investigation unit, helping to solve murder cases. I think his special abilities made it the perfect job for him. I helped him with cases sometimes too, when I had time during school breaks.

My dad swirled the wine around in his glass, thinking about how to answer. Of course, the cases he worked on were confidential, so he had to be careful about what he said about work. "Well, the last case was a real emotional roller coaster. The victim was just a child, seven years old."

I shook my head, realizing that was the same age my students were. "Were they able to find the person who did it?"

He nodded. "That is the best part of the job, bringing justice to the victim's family. It turns out it was a family friend. And the little boy was able to tell me who did it and locate the murder weapon."

There was silence in the air as I thought about how scared the spirit of that child must have felt. But he was still brave enough to help solve his own murder, maybe saving another family from the same heartache.

"Was the child able to cross-over after that?" I asked. Usually when a spirit was able to take care of whatever unfinished business they had here on earth, they could cross over to a much better place.

My dad nodded with a smile. "He was. Right after he said goodbye to his parents and his sister."

Sometimes it was hard for people to believe that we could talk to their deceased loved ones. My dad and I were always treated differently after we told someone about our special abilities, which is why I tried to keep that part of myself a secret. Not many people knew this about me, and I wanted to keep it that way. I had dated a few times in college, but the relationships would quickly end when I told them about my abilities. Most people can't handle everything that goes along with it. It took my mom a long time to feel comfortable when dad and I would discuss our abilities. Her and Freddy didn't share this gift, although I think sometimes, they wished they did.

My dad cleared his throat and took another sip of wine, a cue that he wanted to change the subject. "Thanks again for letting Freddy stay with you. I know he isn't exactly easy right now. Your mom and I are hoping maybe you can get him to open up, get to the bottom of what is going on with him. I mean, I know part of it is just normal teenage rebellion. I just can't help but think there is more going on here."

"I'll see what I can do." I said. "I have some fun things planned for us, if Freddy will go along with them."

Just then, Freddy emerged from the guest room. "Go along with what?"

"Well, I have some surprises in mind, but only if you behave, ok?" I said with a warning in my voice. "Now we should eat, I don't know about all of you, but I am starving."

We had a nice family meal that night, laughing and talking as we ate. Even Freddy seemed to enjoy the potatoes and carrots along with a side salad. He even talked about some of the classes and teachers he hoped to get next year.

"I hear Mr. Fulton is a really tough chemistry teacher, but everyone says they learn a lot from him, so I kind of hope I get him."

Freddy went to the same high school I did, called the Bright Academy. Of course, It had been over six years since I graduated. I tried to remember Mr. Futon, but the name didn't ring a bell. "I don't remember him." I said with a shrug.

"That's because he's new. He just transferred over from another private high school." Freddy said, matter of fact. "Oh, and I wanted you all to know, I've been thinking about going by my middle name, Michael. Fredrick is too formal, Fred sounds too mature, and Freddy just reminds me of that freak Freddy Krueger from those 'Nightmare on Elm Street' movies."

My mother sighed. "You know Fred was your grandfather's name. It's a good name, a strong name, and he would be proud for you to have it."

Freddy Shrugged. "Well, he's not here to know, is he? I never even knew him, so why should it matter?"

My mother sat her fork down on her plate, clearly annoyed. "It matters to me, ok? I know you never knew him, but my dad meant a lot to me, and it means a lot to me that you have his name."

"Maybe he shouldn't have had such a crappy name, then." Freddy said, twisting the knife in my mom's heart.

My mom pushed her plate away, dad put his hand on her shoulder, trying to comfort her. "Now, Rachel, let's not get into a battle before we leave on vacation." He looked over at Freddy, with a warning glare. "We can talk about this more when we get back, ok? But for now, I would love to try some of that lemon meringue your sister made for dessert."

Taking my cue, I stood up and headed toward the fridge, grateful again to have a dad who was also the peacekeeper of the family. "Coming right up."

Later that night after our parents went home, Freddy and I watched Jeopardy!. He was quick at answering most of the questions, which reminded me how smart he was. It was an old repeat episode with Alex Trebek as the host. He looked at the contestants as he read the clue. The category was world leaders.

"He came into power 34 days before FDR and left 19 days after him."

"Who is Adolf Hitler." Freddy chimed in without skipping a beat. A few seconds later a contestant gave the same answer, and it was correct.

"Pretty impressive." I told him. "You knew that before the contestant, and she was a college professor."

He shrugged. "I like history."

"I hope you use that brain power in school, too." I said.

"Sometimes, if it's something interesting that I like." He answered quietly, as if he had more to say.

"Well, mom always said sometimes we have to do things we don't want to do." I told him. "Think of it as jumping through a hoop."

He thought about that for a minute. "Maybe I'm just not cut out for school."

"What makes you say that?"

"Well, the teachers all have it out for me, I swear. I can't do anything right. And most of them had you in their class, so I think they expect me to be like you."

"All you can do is be yourself." I told him.

He stared at the TV screen. It was a commercial break, and as if on cue, an ad came on for our grandparents multi-million-dollar company, Goodwin financial. The trademark singing piggy bank sang the jingle. 'Goodwin financial, we've got what you need.'

"How can I be myself when it's never good enough?" He asked.

"You're always good enough." I told him.

"No, I'm not." He shot back, pounding his fist against his leg. "Don't you get it?"

"Get what?" I asked, trying to understand where my brother was coming from.

"You have everything!" He yelled. "Dad and you both have your ghost whisperer thing in common. You solve murders together and you speak another language. One that mom and I will never understand. I wish I spoke that language, but I don't. So, I feel left out all the time. I feel like I'm always left out and that sucks. I wish I had the connection you and dad have, but I never will. I wish I was a medium too, but I never will be."

I took a deep breath, trying to take in what my brother was saying to me. "Believe me, you don't want the abilities dad and I have. It isn't always easy. It's a blessing, but more than that, it's a curse. There's more to it than just communicating with the dead and solving murders. It means dealing with a lot of deep problems the deceased people have. It means knowing more than you should ever know. And it is heavy, it will weigh on your soul until there isn't much left. I honestly wouldn't wish this gift on my worst enemy, let alone my own brother. So, I'm glad you don't have it. I'm glad you are normal. You should be glad too."

"Well, I'm not!" He said as he stormed into the guest room, slamming the door behind him.

And I was left standing there, feeling more alone and hopeless than I ever had before.

I woke up the next morning with a feeling of dread that was hard to shake. Things were already tense between my brother and I, and it had only been one night. I had dreamed of a wonderful summer where we bonded over lazy days at the beach or the pool, frequented our favorite pizza joint, and laughed and talked until the wee hours in the morning. But it seemed that none of those things were going to happen now. Freddy would be happier spending the entire summer in the guest room, staring at his phone. But I wasn't going to let that happen. Suddenly a light switch flipped on, and I had an idea.

I flipped open my laptop and watched as it came to life. Then I searched for vacation rentals by the beach and watched as the search results popped up on my screen. I was determined to save this summer from certain disaster. I was going to make this a summer to remember. Then I looked at the prices and realized that a Summer to remember might not be one I could afford. Then I scrolled down more and found the perfect spot at an affordable rate.

Adorable 3 room bedroom rental home along the beach of Santa Cruz with private beach access, pool and hot tub. Children and pet's welcome!

When I scrolled through the pictures, it looked like the perfect spot for a little sibling bonding time. Excitement filled my lungs as I clicked *reserve*.

⁂

"Oh, hell no!" Freddy protested when I told him my plans. "I hate the ocean. I think I'm allergic."

I laughed, trying to keep things as light as possible. "You used to love the ocean. Remember all those trips to Santa Cruz when you were a little boy? You used to laugh as you tried to Karate chop the waves. I think I even have a video of you learning to surf. You were having the time of your life."

He shrugged. "I just don't like it anymore, okay?"

"Well, I want you to give it a chance."

"Why?"

"Because I said so!" I snapped.

Freddy rolled his eyes, and I realized I had made the wrong choice of words. I took a deep breath, trying to find the patience to deal with his teenage temper tantrum.

"Because I already paid for it, and there are no refunds." I told him. "And I know how you feel about wasting money."

Freddy sighed. "Fine, I'll go, but I'm not going to be happy about it, okay? This isn't going to be some sort of feel-good sibling bonding trip like you see in the movies or in those stupid novels you like to read."

"We'll see about that." I said, a slight smile forming across my face.

"Whatever." Freddy snorted, pulling his phone out of his pocket. "When do we leave?"

"Tomorrow."

"Are you serious? I was supposed to get together with my friends tomorrow. We go to lunch at Cantina Azteca. It's a tradition we do at the end of every school year."

"Well, how about you reschedule when we get back?" I suggested. "We'll only be gone a week."

He sighed loudly. "I'll see, but we've been planning this for weeks. This beach trip just came up last minute and you expect me to be happy about it?"

"I just expect you to keep an open mind." I told him. "You might even have fun."

"I doubt it." he said, as he walked into the guest room and closed the door behind him.

I let out a long breath of frustration. This summer wasn't going as I planned at all.

CHAPTER

3

"Rise and shine!" I called as I opened the shade in the guest room to let in the morning light. Freddy rolled over and moaned. I knew it would be hard to wake him up since he had been up most of the night playing some video game on his i pad. He had spent most of the day in the guest room, coming out only briefly to eat. But today was a new day, a new beginning. I could feel it in my bones. The fresh ocean air was calling my name, and I wanted to get an early start to beat the traffic. "Come on, Freddy, wake up."

"I'm awake." He mumbled, rolling over to check the time on his phone. "It's way too early."

"Maybe if you'd gone to bed at a decent time like I told you to, you wouldn't be so tired."

"It's summer vacation." He argued. "That's what summer is for. Staying up late and sleeping in."

"Well, I want to leave in an hour, so get your butt out of bed." I suddenly got a very strong whiff of body odor. "Oh, and take a shower. I'll be downstairs making breakfast."

Freddy came down to the kitchen just twenty minutes later, his hair was damp, and he smelled like Old Spice body wash.

"Good morning." I said. "I made waffles, scrambled eggs, and sausage. Well, the sausage is for me since you're vegetarian now." I took a bite, savoring the flavor of the crisp delicious sausage. "You're really missing out, this is good."

"I'm not hungry."

"Breakfast is the most important meal of the day." I pointed out. "And I don't know when we'll be stopping for lunch, so eat up." I pushed a plate toward him, and he sighed as he scooped a small amount of egg onto his plate.

"Is there coffee?"

"Since when do you drink coffee?" I asked, surprised.

"Since you made me wake up so damn early." He snapped, rubbing his eyes.

"Okay, one cup of joe coming up." I said, determined to keep the peace.

Once we had loaded our luggage and snacks in the car, double checked that all of the lights were off and doors were locked, gone back in the house three separate times because one of us forgot something, and once again to use the bathroom one more time, we were ready to hit the road. I punched the address in the GPS on my phone. Two hours and twenty-eight minutes if we drove non-stop.

"Are you sure we have everything?" I asked, adjusting the rear-view mirror.

Freddy sighed. "We're only going to be a few hours away. Whatever we forget, I'm sure we can get it at the store. And I didn't wake up so early for nothing, so let's go."

I slowly backed the car out of the driveway, still feeling like I was forgetting something. But I pressed on, down the street and to the freeway entrance.

"So, we can make a stop in San Francisco if you like, and then Half Moon Bay. That will make it a fun day." I suggested.

Freddy shrugged. "Whatever, you're the one who's driving."

"I definitely want to go the scenic route, down highway 1." I told him. "There's so much to see along the coast."

I watched in the rear-view mirror as Freddy shoved his ear pods into his ears, clearly wanting to drown out the annoying sound of my voice. I rolled my eyes and continued to drive, cranking up the radio to a classic rock station. Freddy continued to stare blankly ahead, oblivious to anything that was going on around him. I sang along to the Beatles song, *Ob-La-Di, Ob-La-Da* at the top of my lungs. It had been one of my great-grandma's favorite songs, and it still brought a smile to my face every time I heard it. Finally, Freddy pulled the ear pods out of his ears.

"Who sings that song?" He demanded.

"The Beatles." I said with a smile, happy to start a conversation about music.

"Let's keep it that way." He said sarcastically, shoving the ear pods back in his ears.

"Oh Brother." I said under my breath. He really wasn't making this easy. And we still had over two hours to go.

The rest of the drive went on without a hitch. We stopped at San Francisco and checked out pier 39 and had lunch at a little café that overlooked the bay. We stopped to look at the iconic sea lions and I commented on how cute they were. Freddy, of course, didn't seem to care.

"All they do is sleep and make that annoying barking sound." he said, plugging his nose. "And they smell horrible."

We also made a quick stop at Half Moon Bay to use the bathroom and stretch our legs before we continued on to our final destination. I was excited to get there, the pictures made it look like an awesome place to stay, and I hadn't been to Santa Cruz in years.

The route down highway 1 was just as beautiful as I remembered, with views of the coast and surrounding mountains. I even saw Freddy look up from his phone briefly to admire the beauty of it all, which filled me with hope that this summer wasn't a lost cause after all. That feeling was only short lived, because when I arrived at the beach house I had rented, it didn't look at all like the pictures in the Airbnb online profile. This place was falling apart, with chipped paint, a roof that seemed to be caving in, and a pool that was half full of green slimy water. I looked back at Freddy, who was fixated on whatever he was doing on his phone.

"We're here."

He looked up, and his face immediately fell into a frown of disbelief.

"This is the place?"

"Yep."

"I thought it had a pool."

I pointed to the disgusting algae filled pool. "I guess that is it."

"Wow, you really know how to pick a winner, sis."

I looked over and realized an older man with silver hair and a well-manicured beard was sitting on the front porch, rocking in a chair and staring into space. I walked over to him; with the profile I had printed on the Airbnb website.

"Excuse me, sir?"

He looked up, with a sad look in his pale blue eyes.

"Excuse what?"

"Well, I, um, I think there has been a mistake. I reserved this house on Airbnb, but it doesn't look anything like it did on the website."

I handed the paper to him, with a look on my face that demanded answers. A look of recognition crossed his face.

"Oh, I told those assholes to take this property off the site. They make things so damn difficult these days with apps and websites and all that garbage. That picture was taken twenty years ago or so, when this house was in its glory. Estelle and I bought it for a vacation home back in the day." He looked at the picture, admiring the way it used to be. "Obviously, it has fallen into disrepair since she died, but when I stay here, I feel like she's with me somehow. So, I stay here most of the time now." He sighed and handed the picture back to me.

"So, you aren't renting the house anymore?" I asked, looking around in disbelief. "I brought my younger brother here so we could enjoy our summer." I gestured toward the car, where Freddy sat with his ear pods in his ears, looking down at his phone. The man looked over at my brother, and back to me.

"Well, I suppose there's enough room. We could all stay together. I have the master bedroom, but there are two other bedrooms you can stay in if you like. Where are you two from, if you don't mind me asking?"

"Sacramento." I answered.

"Well, you didn't drive all this way for nothing, so you might as well stay here with me." The old man said, a crack in his voice. "My name is Ron, by the way, and I'm a Sacramento native myself. What's your name, young lady?"

"Samantha." I answered. "That is my brother, Freddy." I gestured toward the car.

He nodded. "Welcome, Samantha from Sacramento. And your little brother Freddy, too. You guys should make yourselves at home."

I looked around the property, which was clearly falling apart.

"I don't want to impose, sir. Freddy and I can just head back home. Honestly, it would probably be easier than trying to convince my brother to stay here. He's been difficult lately. He's fifteen, and I think hormones have taken over every inch of his body. He didn't want to come to begin with, so he will probably be relieved."

The old man looked toward the car, a slight smile on his face. "Let me talk to him, man to man. After all, I used to be a teenager once."

I laughed. "Maybe you were a teenager once, but I doubt you can convince Freddy to stay here. Let's just say he is difficult to say the least. He will probably look for any excuse to head home and sit in front of his computer for the rest of the summer."

The old man's smile grew brighter.

"Let's just see about that, shall we?"

He walked to the car and started a conversation with Freddy. I couldn't tell what they were talking about, but after a few minutes, Freddy nodded, and retrieved his suitcase from the back seat. Then he walked toward the house with his suitcase in his hand, following the old man inside.

"Freddy, what are you doing?" I whispered.

"Putting my stuff in my room." He said, as if it were obvious.

I could feel my mouth fall into an 'o' of surprise.

"But you didn't want to stay here to begin with. I was sure once you saw this place you would be ready to head home."

He shrugged. "It has a certain appeal."

"With chipped paint, a sagging roof and a pool full of mold?" I asked, surprised.

"I like the owner." He said, matter of fact.

'You only met him for two minutes." I pointed out. "How come when I tried to get you to come, you immediately shot me down, but you talk to this guy, Ron, for two minutes and suddenly you're all for it?" I gestured toward Ron, with a sheepish look on my face. "No offence, sir."

He smiled. "None taken, young lady. I'm just trying to make it up to the two of you for driving all this way. After all, there is plenty of room and I would enjoy the company. This place is lonely since my Estelle died, and I would love to see some life in these walls again. I'll go inside and let you two talk it over. The rooms are available if you want them, and I will make sure there isn't a charge for them, since this clearly wasn't the place you were looking for." He turned and walked inside, leaving Freddy and I to talk it over. It was colder than it was just moments ago, and I began to shiver. I turned toward Freddy; frustration filled my bones.

"What the hell, Freddy? I ask you to come to this beach house with me, and you act like it is a death sentence. But suddenly, this old man asks you to stay, and you're all for it? You need to explain because I am clearly missing something."

He shrugged, a slight smile forming across his face. "Don't you know anything about teenagers?"

"Well, I guess I was one once. And a lot more recently than that old man."

"You should probably read this." He said, pulling a book out of his duffel bag. It was titled 'My life with teenagers.' The cover had a photo of a family with three teenage sons.

"I don't see how this will help." I shook my head.

"Well, this explains where I am at, developmentally. This is the book mom and dad read to try to figure me out. So, I want you to know, all of that reverse psychology bullshit you guys try isn't going to work, because I am already ten steps ahead of you. Also, teenagers always have a better relationship with people they don't consider an authority figure. I don't consider Ron an authority figure."

I sighed. "But I am?"

"I guess. If you say so." He said with a shrug.

"So, you really want to stay here?" I asked in disbelief, looking around at the building in disrepair, and the pool that was growing more mosquitoes by the second.

He nodded. "I really do. Don't ask me why, but I feel like we're meant to be here."

I took a deep breath. "Okay then, let's go tell Ron we're staying."

CHAPTER

I walked into the house with Freddy trailing behind me, on a mission. The old man, Ron sat at an old dining room table, looking like he was defeated.

"Listen," he said. "I know you don't know me, but I am a good person. I am just offering you a place to stay for a few nights or more if you want. I'm sorry the ad did not live up to your expectations, and I am trying to make it up to you. So, Stay, or don't stay. It's completely up to you. But I want you to have that option."

I froze, as if time were standing still, and looked over at my brother, who was staring into space, making it hard to read what he was thinking.

"Do you really want to stay?"

He nodded. "I really do."

"Okay then, we'll stay." I said.

The old man nodded. "Okay, stay as long as you want. Let me show you around. And you just might decide you like it as much as Estelle and I did."

I rolled my eyes, thinking there was no way that was going to happen.

"The living room is that way." He gestured toward a comfortable looking room, with an old sofa and chairs that probably dated to the

1970's, an ancient looking T.V. and coffee table, and wallpaper with a floral pattern that matched the chairs. I immediately felt like I was stepping back in time. He showed us where the kitchen was, of course it was just as outdated with ancient appliances and more floral wallpaper. And then he showed Freddy and I the two guest rooms that were available. They were simple, with a single bed in each room and a dresser, but I thought to myself it would be fine for one night.

After we put our things away in our rooms and used the restroom, which was right across the hall, the three of us debated on what to have for dinner.

"I would cook something for you," Ron said as he rummaged through the fridge, "but I am a terrible cook, and I haven't stocked up the fridge lately since it's only been me. But if you like, there is this great little sea-side bistro down the way. Let me treat you to dinner there. Estelle and I used to go all the time. It serves good fish and chips, hamburgers, and salads, too, since young Freddy is a vegetarian."

I blinked, wondering how the old man already knew Freddy was a vegetarian. That must have been some conversation they had in the car.

"Sounds good." Freddy said, surprising me again at how flexible he was being.

"Ok, great." Ron said. "You're in for a treat. Just let me grab my coat."

It was a short walk down the beach to a place called Harbor Café. We were greeted right away and seated in a nice outdoor spot overlooking the ocean. It was a beautiful view, and the sound of the waves crashing on the shore was relaxing. Freddy ordered a Pepsi, and Ron and I each ordered a glass of red wine.

"So, tell me more about yourselves." Ron said, taking a sip of his wine. "Freddy said he will be starting his sophomore year in the fall?"

Freddy nodded. "I'm not looking forward to the math, but Mr. Newman is the history teacher, he's pretty cool."

"It's great you have a teacher you can relate to." Ron said. "It must be difficult being a young person these days. When I was in school, we didn't have cell phones or social media. You could do something embarrassing, and everybody would forget about it the next week when someone else did something even more embarrassing. But now everything is posted on tik tok or snap chat or whatever you young people are using these days, and nobody forgets."

Freddy nodded. "Yah, it can be that way sometimes. But it's not so bad, I guess."

"Sounds like you have a good head on your shoulders." Ron said as he turned his attention to me.

"And Samantha, what do you do?"

I smiled, thinking of my students. "I teach first grade."

"That must be a challenge." There was a tone of admiration in his voice that made me feel proud.

"It is, but it's also very rewarding."

The waitress took our orders, Freddy had a salad, Ron and I both chose the fish and chips. I thought to myself that we had the same taste in food and wondered what his life had been like. Even though we had just met, he seemed to have such a calm and caring way about him, I was sure that must have come from his parents. Someone so calm and centered must have had exceptional parents, right?

"So, what about you, Ron?" I asked.

"What about me?" There was sarcasm in his voice, so I knew he understood what I meant.

"You know about us, so tell us more about you."

He shook his head. "You don't want to know my story. Its long and boring, it would probably put you to sleep."

"Humor me." I said. "I bet you have an interesting story to tell."

"It's not very interesting." He said with a flick of his hand.

I sat back in my chair and looked him straight in the eye.

"Let us be the judge of that."

He sighed. "Ok, But I don't think it's really that exciting. I guess I should start at the beginning, if you really need to know. I was born July 2nd, 1938. My parents were Tom Cunnings and Annabelle Marshall. My mother died when she gave birth to me, or at least that's what my father told me. I was raised by him and let's just say it wasn't exactly pleasant. He was an alcoholic, drunk all the time. And he was angry, always taking everything out on me. I was used to it; I didn't know anything different. I learned how to take care of myself early on. How to do my own laundry and cook my own meals. I guess that's a bonus, I learned a lot of life skills my peers didn't know. I was also beaten with a belt if I did anything wrong. I was always nervous about making any mistake, no matter how small. I wanted to please him, to make him proud of me. He was my dad after all, and I idolized him, even if he wasn't perfect."

I blinked, thinking that I had already misjudged Ron's family life. I had always been fascinated with the age-old nature versus nurture debate, especially after I studied child development in college as part of my teaching program. This was proof that a good and caring person can emerge from an abusive home. But how? There had to be someone in his life that filled that void that was left by an absent mother and an abusive father. I had also learned in school how important attachment to a primary caregiver is from a young age. The waitress delivered our food, and we all ate quietly for a while until Ron continued his story.

"I didn't really fit in at school, mostly because I wore dirty clothes that were too small for me, and I probably didn't smell too great, either." He laughed. "After all, there was no mother figure telling me to take a shower every day. So, I played by myself on the playground. Nobody seemed to notice until I started third grade. Mrs. Martin was my teacher that year, and she was the most amazing person I had ever met. She truly cared about her students, and it showed. She noticed I was behind in reading, so she would tutor me during lunch break and after school. And she went to the clothes closet at the school to get me some decent clothes that actually fit. She even took care of the free lunch form my father never signed so I could get a free hot lunch every day."

I nodded, thinking that Mrs. Martin must have been that mother figure for him. I hoped that I had an impact on my young students as well, and that they would remember me so vividly when they were 85 years old.

"Mrs. Martin, Anne was her first name, tried to reach out to my father. Of course, he never made it to any parent teacher conferences. I think she knew my home life wasn't the best, but she didn't have any proof since I kept quiet about everything. She started having me over for dinner a few nights a week, and we would work on reading and writing. Pretty soon, I was ahead of my grade level in almost everything. Her husband James was very accepting of me, too. He taught me how to play baseball. We used to spend hours just tossing the ball around. I didn't know it then, But James and Anne had wanted a child for years, but it never happened for them. They used to say I was the son they never had, and I started spending more and more time with them. I don't think my father even noticed. He was probably glad I was out of his hair, anyway."

I took another bite of my food. "It sounds like you were lucky to have them in your life."

"Yeah." Freddy agreed. "If I wasn't doing well in school my teachers would just make me take summer school. I doubt any of them would take the time to tutor me like that."

Ron nodded, taking a sip of his wine. "Yes, they were very special people, and we had a strong bond. Even when I wasn't in her class anymore, we still spent time together. Some of my best memories were with them. But then, the summer before I started sixth grade, Anne told me her husband had a job opportunity in another state. They would be moving soon. I was heartbroken, and I even begged my dad to let them adopt me. I told him they were better parents than he would ever be. Of course, that just made him angry. He said that he was going to put an end to that right then. He said I would not be seeing them anymore. Then he got in his car and drove over to their house. He didn't know it, but I followed him on my bike. It was only about a mile away. When I got there, I watched from a distance as my dad screamed at the Martins that they were overstepping boundaries and I wasn't their son, I was his. He told them they were not to see me anymore, or he would press charges. I hoped they would fight for me; tell him they were petitioning to adopt me. Tell him he wasn't fit to be my father. But they just nodded and agreed. After my dad took off, I ran up to the Martins with tears in my eyes. I begged them to take me with them. I promised I would be good."

Ron let out a deep sigh and paused for a minute, finishing his food as he wiped his eyes with a napkin. I could tell this memory made him emotional. Finally, after a long pause, Freddy said;

"So, did they take you?"

Ron shook his head. "No, they didn't. Mrs. Martin said that I was always good, probably the best thing that ever happened to them, and I would always be in their hearts. But I wasn't their child to take. She told me she would write. We cried and hugged for a long time before she told me I had to go home."

We were all silent, trying to take it all in. Ron must have felt so alone, with nobody else but his father.

"That must have been rough, losing your only support system at such a young age." I said quietly.

He nodded. "It was. But what doesn't kill us makes us stronger, right? Anyway, I think we should grab the check. Unless anyone wants dessert? They have a delicious brownie cake with vanilla ice cream."

I shook my head. "I'm stuffed. But we would like to hear the rest of your story. What happened after the Martins left?"

He smiled. "That's when I met her. But let's finish my story at home, alright? This old man is getting tired."

Later that night, the three of us sat out on Rons porch, eating a slice of the brownie cake which we'd decided to take to go. He was right, it was really good. I took another bite as I looked out at the ocean, admiring the beauty of it all.

"It really is a spectacular view." I commented. "You're lucky to wake up to this every day."

"I know. I've always felt peaceful here. It really is my happy place. Some of my best days were spent right here." He said quietly. "Now where was I? oh yeah. The Martins moved away, and my dad's abuse got worse after that. Maybe it was because I was getting old enough to stand up to him, but I still wasn't big enough to win any physical battle. I just stayed out of the house as much as I could. I built a little tree fort in a wooded area near my house from scraps the lumber yard would give me. It became my refuge when things got really heated with my father, and it was in such a hidden area, he never knew where I was at. So, I was safe. I started middle school, and it was even harder socially than elementary school. The bullies that used to torture me were bigger and meaner. I became depressed. My grades started to show it, too. But then she moved in next door."

"Estelle?" I asked, mesmerized by his story.

He nodded. "She had hazel eyes and fiery red hair with a personality to match. I thought she was the most beautiful thing I had ever seen. I tried to introduce myself, but I was so nervous I just stuttered. She never laughed at me though. She told me her name was Estelle, and she introduced me to her parents and her older brother, John. We became fast friends. We walked to school together every day and did our homework together. She was smart, and she helped me catch up on the subjects I was behind in. For the first time, I didn't have to eat my lunch alone. She was always by my side. She was my person. One day, when the bullies at school tried to gang up on me, Estelle told them they'd better leave me alone, or else. They laughed at her, of course, and pushed her to the ground. I told her to let it go, and I told them to leave her alone. I felt powerless because I couldn't make them stop. And then her brother came up behind her, all six feet four and muscle. He told them to leave his sister and me alone, or he would pound them until there was nothing left of them. They never bothered me again after that. I finally found a family where I belonged. Estelle's family invited me over for dinner often, and we were inseparable." He smiled, reliving his memories. "Her dad and her brother gave me the third degree when we started officially dating, but they finally came around. I think they knew they could trust me, and I would never do anything to hurt her. Anyway, we dated all the way through high school. We were even prom King and queen. It was a special night. I took her to a fancy restaurant to celebrate, something I'd saved up for with money mowing people's yards and doing odd jobs. I brought her a bouquet of her favorite flowers, snapdragons. That was the night I told her I loved her, and she said she loved me too. Everything was right with the world. Until everything changed, and life took us in separate directions."

"What happened after high school?" Freddy asked. "I mean, you ended up together, right?"

Ron yawned. "Can we continue this story tomorrow? I'm tired, it's way past my bedtime."

"OK." I said. "I guess we can stay one more night. If it's alright with Freddy."

Freddy shrugged. "It's ok with me, if it's ok with Samantha. She's the driver."

"Alright." Ron said, with a satisfied smile on his face. "We will continue my story tomorrow. Same time, same place. Now, we should all get a good night's sleep."

Sometime in the middle of the night I woke up to the sound of someone crying. It sounded like a woman. I slowly got out of bed and crept out to the kitchen, where the sound was coming from, and I saw the silhouette of a woman, standing at the counter and looking out the window as she wept. This was a spirit; I could always tell because they had a certain glow around them. And I could only guess whose spirit it was.

"Estelle?" I whispered.

She turned around to face me, disbelief across her face. She was as beautiful as Ron had described her, although her red hair had now turned a soft silver. "You can see me?"

I nodded. "Clear as day."

"But how?"

"I'm what they call a medium." I explained. "I was born with the gift to communicate with people who have passed away. Usually, I help them with unfinished business. My name is Samantha."

Hope spread across her face. "So, you can help me, Samantha?"

"Yes." I said. "Probably. Ron was telling us about you, how you met when you were kids. I guess you're one of those rare first and only love stories. The kind everyone wants."

She laughed. "It wasn't always smooth sailing though. Ron was such a sweet kid, but he was never very good with words. Especially when it came to saying how he felt." Estelle paused for a moment, reminiscing. "I remember the first day he came to introduce himself when my family moved next door. He was such a nervous mess he could barely get his words out. But I thought he was adorable."

I smiled. "He seems like a nice man. And he looks so young for his age."

Her smile was clouded with worry and concern. "Yes, he does. I don't know if he told you this, but he's very sick."

I shook my head. "No, he didn't. But we just met him today. I guess that's not something you blurt out when you first meet someone. How sick is he?"

She looked out the window again. "Stage 4 pancreatic cancer. Terminal. He only has weeks left, if that. He is no longer seeking treatment. He came here to die."

I took a deep breath. "I'm sorry to hear that. I never would have known."

She nodded. "He's good at masking it. But he's afraid, and so am I."

"What are you afraid of, Estelle?"

Fresh tears started to fill her eyes. "I just don't want him to die alone."

I was taken aback. Surely, there had to be some family, somewhere. "Is there someone I could call? Is that what you need me to do?"

She shook her head. "No. There's no one. All of our family is already gone. There were some friends, but they're scattered all over the place, and probably too old to travel, anyway."

"Did you have children?" I asked, realizing that was a personal question.

"I'll let Ron tell you about that." She said softly. "It's hard for me to talk about."

I nodded, realizing what she wanted me to do. "Okay. So, you want me to stay here with Ron, until he dies?"

She nodded. "Yes, that's exactly what I want. The thought of him dying here alone is more than I can take."

I took a deep breath. "I will try my best. But I do have a job to get back to eventually. And Freddy starts school mid-August."

She started to cry again, and my heart went out to her. I put a gentle hand on her shoulder to comfort her, but it was more like touching air.

"Please don't let him die alone." She begged through her tears.

"Alright." I said. "I will stay with him."

Her eyes brightened again, and she smiled. "Thank you."

CHAPTER

5

The next morning, I woke up to the sound of hammering. I looked at the clock and saw that it was eight-fifteen, so I slipped on some clothes, brushed my teeth and hair and splashed some water on my face to help me wake up. Then I went out to investigate where the sound was coming from. To my surprise, Freddy and Ron were working together to replace some shingles on the house. It was hard for me to comprehend that Ron was so close to dying, he seemed so full of life. And he looked happy as he instructed Freddy on what to do.

"Good morning." I said, loud enough to get their attention.

"Morning." They both said in unison.

"Freddy, you're awake before noon?" I teased.

He shrugged. "I heard Ron out here working, and I figured he needs help."

"There's coffee in the kitchen if you want some." Ron added. "And I put out some cereal and muffins if you like. They say breakfast is the most important meal of the day."

I went in to pour myself some coffee and came back out to watch as they worked. My mind was heavy as I thought of what I could do to help Ron prepare for the end of his life. Freddy had taken a liking to him too, so I was sure he would take it hard. And I was reminded again that my gift was a blessing and a curse. If I hadn't been able to communicate with Estelle, I would have never known Ron was dying. We would have left him there to die alone. The thought made me shiver, and I decided to go for a walk along the beach to clear my head.

The sand felt cool under my feet, and the sound of the waves was relaxing as I walked along the beach. I could see why Estelle loved it here so much. I scooped up a couple of shells to add to my collection and skipped a few rocks as I walked along. There was no one in sight, and I thought that later in the afternoon it would probably be full of people. And then I heard a sound. It was faint at first, but it got louder as I walked closer to where it was coming from. It was the sound of a child crying.

"Hello?" I called. "Is someone there?"

When there was no answer, I kept following the sound. And finally, hiding behind a fallen tree, was a young boy, maybe five or six. He was crying quiet tears. I looked around, but there was no adult in sight.

"Hi." I said. "Are you lost?"

He nodded, his sobs becoming more frantic.

"How old are you?"

He held up 5 fingers.

"Don't be scared. I'm here to help. What's your name?"

"Mathew."

"That's a nice name. I'm Samantha. So, do you know where your mom is, Mathew?"

He shook his head. "I'm here with my dad. I just wanted to go for a little walk, but then I couldn't find him." His sobs started in again, full force.

"Don't worry, I'll help you find your dad. Where do you think you saw him last?"

Mathew shrugged. "I don't know."

I scanned the beach again, but there was no one in sight.

"Well let's walk down this way a little bit to see if we can find your dad." I said.

"But I'm not supposed to go with strangers." He wailed. "I want my daddy!"

"I know you do." I said with a calm and reassuring tone. "I'm just trying to help you. Maybe if I tell you about myself, I won't seem like such a stranger. I'm a teacher, and I teach first grade."

His eyes lit up. "I'll be in first grade in the fall."

"That's great!" I told him in a cheerful voice. "First grade is so much fun. You will learn so much. What's your favorite book, Mathew?"

"*Good night, Moon.*" He answered, now hiccupping between his words. "My dad reads it to me every night."

"That's a good one." I said. "I used to read it to my brother when he was a little boy."

He looked surprised. "Really? That book must be really old."

I laughed at his perception of *really old.* Then I heard someone in the distance calling Mathew's name. The little boy perked up right away.

"Daddy, I'm over here!" He called, waving his hands as fast as he could.

The voice became clearer as he walked closer, and when he spotted his son, his walk became more of a jog. He had dark hair, just like Mathew, and He looked much younger than I had pictured him in my mind. Maybe a year or two older than me, which was young to be the father of a five-year old. He scooped his son up in his arms and embraced him before he gave him a stern look.

"I've told you not to wander off like that!" He said, with more fear than anger in his voice.

"I'm sorry, Daddy. I just wanted to take a little walk, and I didn't mean to go so far. I was trying to find more shells for my collection. I was hiding behind that tree because I was so scared, but then this nice lady found me. I know I'm not supposed to talk to strangers, but I don't think she's a stranger anymore. I already know her name is Samantha, she's a teacher, and she used to read *Goodnight Moon* to her brother."

He looked at me and smiled. He had nice brown eyes that seemed to tell a story.

"Thank you so much for staying with him. He must have been scared; he's not used to being separated from me these days. We're a team, aren't we, buddy?"

Mathew nodded. "Like Batman and Robin."

He tussled his son's hair and hugged him tight again. Then he turned to me. "I'm Charlie, and I take it you know Mathew. Thanks again for staying with him, Samantha. I couldn't take it if anything happened to him, he's really all I have, ever since his mother died."

I was taken aback, His mother must have been so young. I wanted to ask more questions, but decided it really wasn't my business anyway. So, after a beat of silence, I changed the subject. "It's really no problem. I'm just glad you found him. Anyway, I should probably get going, and let the two of you have some father-son time."

"Do you have to go?" Mathew said with an adorable little pout. "I want to show you my rock collection."

I was caught off guard. What started as a quiet walk to clear my head had turned into something else entirely.

"Now Mathew, be polite." Charlie warned. "Maybe she has plans today."

Mathew looked at me, curious. "Do you have plans?"

"Don't put her on the spot like that, son." Charlie said, giving me an apologetic look.

"Sorry." Mathew said, disappointed.

"But maybe," Charlie continued, "If she is free tomorrow, we could treat her to dinner. There's a great little café down the way. And I would love to pay her back for finding you."

The little boys' eyes lit up. "Yah, you should come! They have really good chicken fingers!"

I smiled, wanting to accept the invitation. But then I thought of Ron. He seemed alright now, but what if he took a turn for the worse? Charlie seemed to pick upon my hesitation.

"No pressure though." He added.

"None taken." I replied, thinking to myself that no one could possibly go downhill that fast in a day. And something inside me didn't want to disappoint Mathew any more than his dad. So, I smiled at both of them. "I'd love to go."

⌒∞⌒

By the time I made it back to the house, the late morning sun was shining on Freddy and Ron, who were now painting the trim of the house white. I was impressed at how it really brightened up the house, and made it look new somehow. I was equally impressed with how much progress they had made. I knew that if we'd been at home, Freddy would still be in bed.

"It looks great." I complimented.

"Thanks." Ron said. "It helps to have a young set of hands. Did you have a nice walk?"

I nodded. "Yes, I did. It really is beautiful here."

Ron nodded. "I agree. And I've met some of the nicest people just walking on the beach."

I thought about Charlie and Mathew, and our date the next day. But then I reminded myself that this wasn't a date. It was simply a thank you dinner, and after tomorrow I probably wouldn't see them again.

"Anyway," Ron continued. "I was thinking we could go to the store this afternoon, to get some food in the house that you and Freddy will like. And tonight, I can make spaghetti for dinner. It's the one meal I can make that is edible."

"Are you sure you're up to that?" I asked.

"Of course." He said, so confidently that I knew there was no arguing with him.

So, after he and Freddy finished painting the trim and washed up, we went to a cute little grocery store down the way where we stocked up on snacks and drinks, eggs and milk and all the supplies Ron would need to cook spaghetti, with meatballs on the side. We `also picked up some sandwiches from the deli for lunch that day. After we got home and unpacked the groceries, Ron went out to put a few last touches on the trim of the house. I watched him from the window, amazed that he seemed to be doing so well, considering his diagnosis. I wondered if Estelle could have been wrong, if maybe she'd misunderstood. But she seemed so sure that Ron had come here to die. I was deep in thought when Freddy came up behind me.

"So, are we just staying one more night?" Freddy asked, following my gaze to Ron, who set his paintbrush down and stepped back to inspect his work.

"Well, I wanted to talk to you about that." I said. "Something has come up, and Ron might need us to stay longer than that."

"What came up?" Freddy asked.

"Well, I woke up in the middle of the night, and I spoke to the spirit of his wife, Estelle."

Freddy laughed. "So, not only is this place falling apart, its haunted, too? This summer just keeps getting better. So, what did his dead wife say?"

"She said Ron is dying." I answered.

Freddy shook his head. "He seems fine to me."

I shrugged. "That's what she told me. And she doesn't want him to die alone."

"So, isn't there some family out there we can call? He must have grandkids, right?"

"Estelle said there is no one. And she wants us, or at least me, to stay with him."

"I don't see why this has to be on us." Freddy said. "We barely know the guy."

"I know." I told him. "But I want to let her spirit rest in peace. I know it's hard to understand."

Freddy looked around the kitchen. "Is she here right now?"

I shook my head. "Spirits only show themselves to me when they want to. I'm sure I will see her again tonight."

He nodded. "Did she say how long he has?"

"A few weeks at the most." I answered. "But it's hard to predict."

"Ok, well, if he's still alive when school starts, does that mean we get to extend our summer break?" Freddy asked with hope in his voice.

"We'll cross that bridge when we get to it." I said. "Right now, I think we should get ready for lunch. It's been a long morning, and I'm starved."

We had our sandwiches for lunch, turkey for Ron and I, cheese and tomato for Freddy, and spent the rest of the afternoon at the beach. We walked along as the waves splashed our ankles, and before long, Freddy dove right in, body surfing on the waves just like he did when he was younger. Ron laughed, and my heart melted to see him enjoying himself. After all, that's what this little road trip was all about.

About halfway down the beach was when I noticed Ron clutching his chest. This was the first time I had seen him in pain, so I was obviously concerned.

"Are you alright?" I asked, rushing to his side.

"Oh, I'm fine." He said with a flick of his hand. "Just getting old is all. Why don't you two go on without me. I want you to enjoy yourselves. I'll only slow you down."

With that, he turned and walked back to the house, a little slower than usual.

That night, Ron made a delicious spaghetti dinner with garlic bread and salad, which we all enjoyed. He called it his *one hit wonder,* claiming it was the only decent meal he knew how to make. After that, we all sat out on the front porch, where Ron continued his story.

"Estelle was my high school sweetheart, and we loved each other very much. It made some of the other guys jealous, they all wanted a chance with the popular and charming Estelle, Especially Bill Frank, captain of the football team. But she loved me. Our senior year, we used to spend a lot of time at the beach. We would spend a lot of weekends right here. We would have picnics, look up at the stars, and make out in my car." He laughed. "Those were the good old days. One night, after a football game, I went to the snack bar to get some drinks, and when

I turned around, Estelle was gone. My heart was racing until I finally found her in the back of Bill Franks car. He was on top of her, trying to have his way with her. She was trying to push him away, telling him to stop. I'm usually not a fighter but seeing my Estelle in danger made my adrenaline pump. I yanked him out of the car and socked him right in the eye, hard. I had never seen the captain of the football team scared, but he ran off with his tail between his legs. I scooped Estelle up in my arms and promised her I wouldn't let anyone hurt her again."

Freddy shook his head in disbelief. "I can't believe you fought the captain of the football team and won."

Ron smiled. "A man will do crazy things for love. You'll see someday, when you meet your person."

Freddy shook his head and made a face. "I plan on being a bachelor for life. Women are way too complicated. It isn't worth the stress."

"You may feel different in a few years." Ron said with a chuckle. "Anyway, Estelle and I both graduated with honors. The only difference was, she had money to go to college, and I didn't. I never wanted to hold her back, so I was excited for her when she decided to go to the university of San Diego to pursue her teaching credential. After all, it was only nine hours away, and a quick flight from Sacramento. I got a job working at an automotive store. My goal was to save up enough money to move to San Diego to be with Estelle. We used to talk on the phone every day, and send letters all the time, through snail mail. This was before E mail was a thing, and I used to run out to the mailbox to get her letters. I wanted to go see her, but my job kept me so busy it was hard to find time. Pretty soon, the letters were few and far between, and the phone calls became brief. I told myself Estelle was just busy with school, but deep down, I knew there was more to it. Her family had moved away, so I had lost touch with them, too. I still lived in my dad's house, technically, but he was hardly ever home, and when he was, we rarely said more than a few words to each other, which was fine with me. But one day, I got a letter that changed everything."

"Was it from Estelle?" I asked, assuming the obvious.

He shook his head and walked into the house to retrieve what appeared to be a book full of pictures and letters. He pulled out one handwritten letter and handed It to me.

"I get emotional reading this, so I'll let you do the honors."

I cleared my throat as I started to read.

Dearest Ron,

We don't know where to begin, except to say we are so sorry for leaving you that night. You must have felt so frightened and alone. We could tell you were afraid of your father, and so were we. We didn't know what we could have legally done to make you our son, but looking back on that night, if we could go back in time, we would scoop you up and run far far away to start a new life, free from your father and his abuse. We would have loved you as our own and given you the best life we possibly could. It's too late for that now, but hopefully we can still have a positive effect on your life. Now that you are legally an adult, there is nothing stopping you from coming to see us in New York. We would love to see you and we have included our contact info, along with a special gift. Look at it as a belated high school graduation gift to the son we never had.

Love always

James and Anne Martin

I sat the letter down, a little misty eyed. "What was the gift?"

Ron looked up; his eyes were moist too. "A check. Enough to fly to New York to see them, put myself through college, and still have a down payment for my own apartment. Enough to change my life. I called them and thanked them; they were both so happy that I had received the letter. They were afraid my dad might intercept it. So, I made the flight plans, told my boss I was taking an extended vacation, which I really enjoyed because he was a jerk anyway. I had never been out of California, and New York was magical. The buildings were so tall. I stayed with the Martins for about a week, and it felt like we had never been apart. They showed me the big city, we spent a lot of time walking around and catching up. Anne was still teaching third grade, and James worked at the university. He gave me a tour; I think they hoped I would go to school there and stay with them. But I wanted to see Estelle. It had been weeks since we had talked, and she never seemed to pick up the phone. And I knew I had enough money to do that now, thanks to the Martins. So, I booked a flight to San Diego."

"I bet Estelle was glad to see you." I said with a smile. But Rons eyes just went dark, pain and hurt across his face.

"She was surprised, to say the least." I brought a bouquet of her favorite flowers, and I couldn't wait to see her again, to hold her in my arms. But when I showed up at her dorm room, I could tell right away that something was off. She said how surprised she was to see me, but she wished I had warned her first. I told her I wanted to surprise her. Then I told her how I had reconnected with the Martins, and how they wanted to help me start a better life for myself. I said I wanted to move to San Diego and go to school and get an apartment. That I wanted to start a life with her. And that's when she started crying."

"Tears of joy?" I mused.

Ron shook his head, and I could tell he was going to cry any minute. "No. She had met someone she felt was a better fit for her. She said she was trying to find a way to tell me. That she had written at least ten letters but never sent them. That our lives were just too different. I told her it didn't have to be that way anymore. That I loved her. I begged her to change her mind. But in the end, I just wanted her to be happy, even if it wasn't with me."

"So that's it?" Freddy asked. "You just gave up? And what was with her even dating someone else when you were supposed to be together? Now I know I want to be single forever. That is just way to depressing."

Ron sighed. "Nobody ever said love was easy. We cried and hugged each other for hours before I grabbed a cab and headed to the airport. I already knew I wanted to move to New York to be with the Martins. But I had one stop to make first. I booked the first flight back to Sacramento. I needed to see my father one more time. He was the same angry drunk he always was, asking where I had been and demanding to know where I was going when he saw me packing the rest of my things. I told him it was none of his business. That I was an adult now and I was going to start a life of my own. He asked how I could do that when I was a loser with no money and no drive. I said he was the worst father on the planet, and I wished he would rot in hell. We got in a huge fight, but now I was bigger than him. For the first time, he couldn't overpower me. So, in the end, I grabbed my things, and headed out of my childhood home, never looking back. Of course, The Martins welcomed me with open arms. James used his weight to get me enrolled in the university, and I even got a job working in the office. I never knew exactly what I wanted to do, so I started with all of my prerequisites. My life was finally on track. It was just missing one thing."

"Estelle." I whispered.

Ron nodded, with another pool of tears forming in his eyes. "I wrote her a letter. I told her I was in New York, going to school and working. I hoped she was happy too. That I would always love her, and if she ever needed me, I would be there."

"Did she write back?" I asked.

He shook his head. "No. So I assumed she was happy. I kept busy with my job and school. Even went on a few dates, but nobody special. Nobody like Estelle."

"But you ended up together eventually, right?" I asked, hopefully.

He smiled. "Maybe. But that is to be continued tomorrow. It's this old man's bedtime."

That night after everyone was in bed, Estelle's spirit came to visit me again. She seemed more relaxed this time, more at peace somehow. I saw her sitting in a chair near the bedroom window, looking out at the ocean.

"I'm glad Ron has been telling you our story." She said.

"Me too." I agreed. "Although I thought it was sad that you dumped him for some other guy in college. Just out of curiosity, did you ever receive the letter he sent?"

She nodded. "I did. But I was stubborn and set my ways. Anyway, I will let Ron tell you the rest of that story. I had a question for you, though."

"What's that?" I asked, muffling a yawn.

"Well, I wondered if you could help me talk to him. Be our interpreter of sorts."

I took a deep breath, choosing my words carefully.

"I don't know how Ron feels about the afterlife. But I must warn you some people have a hard time believing me when I say I'm a medium. Some people are even angry."

She nodded. "I understand. And he might feel that way at first. But if I tell you some things that only he and I would know, I think he would come around. It would mean a lot to me if I could just talk to him, even one more time. I think it would mean a lot to him too."

"Okay." I said, not wanting to disappoint her. "We will do it tomorrow."

CHAPTER

6

The next morning, I woke up to the sound of hammering again. After I splashed water on my face and brushed my teeth and hair, I poured myself a cup of coffee and walked out to the side of the house where I found Ron and Freddy working on the filter to the swimming pool.

"Morning." I said.

"Good morning, Samantha." Ron answered. "I thought we would try to get this pool up and running again. I've been meaning to do this for a while now. I used to enjoy a good swim after a day at the beach. It's a good way to wash all the saltwater and sand off, and its calm and relaxing."

"Well, let me know if you need any help." I told him.

"I think young Freddy and I have it handled." He said with a wink. "Thanks for the offer. You should take a walk. It's a beautiful morning."

I took Rons advice and took a walk along the beach, sipping my coffee and kicking the sand as I walked along. I had a million thoughts racing through my mind when I felt my cell phone vibrating in my pocket. I was relieved when I saw it was my dad. If anyone could understand what I was going through, it was him.

"Hi, Dad." I answered.

"Hey Sammy girl. Just calling to check up on Freddy. Hope he's not giving you too much trouble."

"No, not at all." I said. "He's been doing great. We're spending the week in Santa Cruz. I found a little house on the beach."

"That sounds like fun." He said. "Freddy used to love the beach. Lately it's hard to get him out of his room."

"I know what you mean." I said with a chuckle. "He fought me at first, but I think it's been good for him. Anyway, dad, I could really use some advice. Medium to medium."

His voice became serious. "What's going on?"

"Well, the beach house is owned by this nice old man, his name is Ron. He has been telling us his life story, and it's fascinating. The problem is the spirit of his wife is also here. She told me he has stage 4 cancer, and he came here to die. Since he has nobody, she wants me to stay with him, so he doesn't have to die alone. And now she wants me to help them communicate. The only problem is, I don't know how he'll respond."

My dad paused for a minute, taking this all in. "Wow, that's heavy."

"That's an understatement." I whispered.

"Well, the only thing you can do is just be yourself." He said. "You can't control how people will react when you share your gift with them. You can only control how you present it. If you speak from the heart, most people will come around, even if they are cynical at first."

I nodded, feeling grateful to have a dad who understood me so well. "That makes sense."

"You're a smart girl. You'll know what to do. After all, you are my daughter."

I smiled. "Thanks dad. "So how are things in Paris?"

"Wonderful. We saw the Eiffel tower, went on a day tour of the city, and tomorrow night we have a dinner cruise."

"Sounds great." I said.

"Thank you again for making it possible." I could tell by his voice he meant it. "And I'm glad you and Freddy are having a good time too."

"We really are."

"Well, mom wants to say hi too. And Sammy?"

I paused, waiting for him to finish.

"I'm always here. If you ever need to talk. No matter how old you get, you're always my little girl."

I felt my heart melt, and more relaxed than I had felt just minutes before. "I know."

Later that morning, after Ron and Freddy had finished working on the pool, we all sat around it, watching it fill up. I noticed that Ron looked paler than he did earlier, and his breathing was rapid too. Of course, he assured me that he was alright. We all had a late morning breakfast of bacon, eggs and potatoes, and then we sat on the porch, looking out at the ocean while Ron continued his story.

"Like I said, I never knew exactly what I wanted to do, but I was always interested in music, so I majored in that for a while. I had a permanent job at the NYU office, which wasn't that exciting, but it did give me a paycheck. I was saving up to get my own apartment, but something was comforting about living with the Martins. I think I was probably reliving the childhood I never had. I must admit it was kind of nice to have someone do my laundry and cook dinner for me. I'd never had that before. And I think they enjoyed having me around, too. So, for the next five years, that's what I did. My life was great, but I never stopped thinking about Estelle. Then one day, I found out through a mutual friend that she was getting married. It was going to be a big event in Lake Tahoe. I told myself that I shouldn't interfere. After all, Estelle was happy, and that's all that mattered to me. But in the end, I needed closure at least. So, I booked a flight and a hotel stay near the event. And I stood in the back that day, watching her say her vows to another man."

"But you stopped her, right?" Freddy interrupted. "I mean it's obvious the two of you were meant to be together."

Ron just shook his head. "She looked so happy, and like I said, that's all that really mattered to me. So, I flew home that afternoon."

I noticed Estelle's spirit sitting beside him, listening to every word. She looked sad, too. "Only I wasn't so happy. I thought about Ron every day."

"I thought of her every day." Ron echoed. "But I didn't think there was anything I could do about it. I moved on with my life. But then, one year later, when I was upstairs reading, Anne came in to tell me someone was there to see me, and I couldn't believe my eyes. It was Estelle. She was still beautiful, but she looked sad. And soon after that, I noticed the bruises. She ran into my arms, and she was trembling. James and Anne went out to grab a bite to eat and see a movie so we could talk. She told me that her husband, Greg, had been beating her. It started shortly after they were married. I was livid. I wanted to go and kill him with my own bare hands. But she told me he was already in jail. It turns out, she never stopped thinking about me either. She said she was sorry she ever thought anyone else could make her as happy as I did. I told her I was sorry too. After all, I had promised her I would never let anybody hurt her again, and I did. Estelle just assured me that there was no way I could have known. That now, we could only move forward. And we agreed that we wanted to be together. We made love that night, and we were never apart again. Well, at least until she died."

Estelle looked at me signaling for me to tell Ron that she was here. Of course, I was still nervous about how he would react. But I took a deep breath and spat it out.

"What if I told you she's here right now."

His eyes widened. "What? Is this some kind of joke?"

I shook my head. "I wouldn't joke about something like this. I'm a medium, I can speak to people who have passed away. Estelle came to me a few nights ago. She's worried about you."

Ron sighed. "I've never believed in that sort of thing. I always thought that when you're gone, you're gone."

"Sometimes the deceased have unfinished business." I told him. "And when they do, I can help them cross over."

"She really can." Freddy said. "I've seen her do it. It's amazing."

Estelle leaned closer to Ron. "I'm right here, love."

I could tell Ron was still skeptical, and so could Estelle.

"Ask him to tell you about the engagement ring." She said. "It was beautiful platinum, and the diamonds were shaped like a flower. And he dropped it when he was proposing to me on the beach. A wave came up and washed it away, I thought we would never find it. He was so upset that he sifted through the sand for hours until he finally found it. He was so proud. He said even if he'd bought another ring for me, it wouldn't be that ring."

I repeated what Estelle had said, and Ron looked at me, shocked.

"How did you know that? Have you been going through my things?"

"No, I swear Estelle told me to tell you that."

"She really is here?" he said, his voice cracking with emotion.

I nodded, tears forming in my eyes. "She's standing right beside you."

Ron looked up, as if he could see her. "Hello darling."

Estelle beamed. "Hello, my love."

That night, I made the short walk down to Harbor café to meet Charlie and Mathew for dinner. My emotions were all over the place after the reunion between Ron and Estelle. There was such a beautiful bond between the two of them, the kind of love I hoped for someday. But the rational side of me knew that was one in a million. No one loves each other that much.

When I arrived, the two were already waiting for me, at a nice outdoor table facing the beach.

"Samantha!" Mathew screeched as he ran up and gave me the biggest hug, which melted my heart. His dad stood behind him, grinning from ear to ear. He was wearing jeans with a nice polo shirt, matching

Mathews' outfit, and I thought to myself that he looked handsome, even more than he had the day before.

"Thanks for coming out to meet us." Charlie said.

"Thanks for inviting me." I said, meaning it.

We all sat together that night, ordering our favorite foods, chicken fingers for Mathew and salads for Charlie and me. Charlie and I both ordered the blonde beer, and Mathew ordered a root beer. The food was amazing, and the company was even better.

"Did you know these are the best chicken fingers on the planet?" Mathew asked, taking a bite of his chicken finger, with a big smile on his face.

"I didn't know that." I said. "Do you think the steak salad is good, too?"

Mathew made a face. "I don't know, because I don't eat salad. But dad says its good, so I believe him."

Charlie smiled. "It is pretty good."

"I believe your dad." I said, taking a bite of my salad. "It is pretty good."

There was a relaxed silence between the two of us as we ate. I felt a comfortable connection that I hadn't felt for a long time.

"So, Samantha, how long will you be here in Santa Cruz?" Charlie asked.

The question was innocent but filled me with so many emotions.

"I'm not sure." I said. "Maybe a few weeks? My younger brother and I came here for vacation, but we might be staying longer than we anticipated. There is a family friend who is sick, and he might need us a little longer."

Charlie's face was full of emotion, and curiosity. "Well, I hope your friend gets well soon."

"Me too." I said, meaning it.

"So, you said you have a younger brother." Charlie continued. "How old is he, if you don't mind me asking."

"Fifteen." I answered. "His name is Freddy. I tried to plan this trip as a sibling bonding vacation. Our parents are in Paris, and I wanted to give them a break, so I booked this vacation for my brother and me. I think it is working so far, and Freddy is having fun. But I just wonder if it's worth it, you know?"

Charlie smiled. "I think I know exactly what you mean. I planned this vacation for Mathew and I, but I'm not sure if it's the right time. His mother died about a year ago, so I thought we needed to get away. Now I'm not so sure. The house we're staying at is a vacation house we bought together after Mathew was born. There are so many memories of her here. We both miss her so much, but I know it's time to move on. I'm just not sure how to do that."

I took a deep breath, not sure how to answer his question. So, I answered the only way I knew how. "When the time is right, I'm sure you will find the answer."

He smiled, looking over at his son. "I think we will too."

After a fantastic dinner, the three of us took a walk on the beach, where Charlie and I had the chance to talk while Mathew collected rocks and shells.

"Thank you again for staying with Mathew." Charlie said. "I honestly can't imagine if something had happened to my little boy."

The thought seemed to give him shivers, as his body shook as he said the words.

"It's no problem." I said. "Any honest person would have done the same thing."

"But any honest person isn't you." Charlie Said, answering so raw and full of truth I had to step back for a moment.

"I wouldn't just trust Mathew with anyone." He continued. "But when I saw him with you, I knew he was safe somehow. Like I didn't have to worry anymore."

I looked at Mathew, who was throwing rocks into the ocean. "I just wanted to protect him. I knew he was scared, and I wanted him to find his mom, or dad."

Charlie looked over at Mathew, thinking about what to say next.

"I met his mom, Grace, when we were in college. She was getting her teaching credential and I was getting my business degree. We had an instant connection, but kids weren't in our near future. We both had a five-year plan and that did not include Mathew. But after a crazy frat party we found out she was pregnant. We were both scared, but we accepted it, and we were excited to welcome our son into the world. Our families and friends all thought we were crazy. They said there was no way we were ready to be parents. But before we knew it Mathew was born, and he was the best thing that ever happened to us."

As if on cue, Mathew picked up a rock and examined it. "Hey, daddy, I think I found a new rock for my collection! It's white and full of sparkles!"

"It looks great son!" Charlie gushed, without missing a beat. Then, he turned back to me.

"Like I said, he was the best thing that ever happened to his mom and me. Grace loved being a mom and I loved being a dad. He really was the best baby. He never cried, he just smiled, this big bright smile, the one he still has today. Grace loved him so much; she really was the best mom. She played with him and took him to Storytime at the library and playdates at the park. Then one day, about a year ago, she went to the grocery store, just like she did every week. I was home with Mathew, because he hated being in a car seat, and it went so much faster when he wasn't with us, so we usually took turns. I still remember the yellow sundress she was wearing that day. It was one of her favorites. Anyway, she got the groceries, and on her way home, she was hit dead on by a drunk driver, killed instantly. The police came to my house to tell me what had happened. I didn't believe them. I told them they were lying; they were full of shit. But it was the truth. It was my reality. And it was Mathew's reality."

"I'm so sorry." I said, meaning it.

"Its okay." He answered. "It's just life. Anyway, I don't want to depress you, this is supposed to be a fun night. So enough about me. I'd like to hear more about you."

I laughed, making little circles in the sand with my feet. "Theres not too much to tell. I'm a first-grade teacher in Sacramento, and I think that's always what I wanted to do. It's very rewarding, and the summers off are a huge plus."

Charlie nodded. "Yah, that would be nice. I do data entry for a medical insurance company. Most of my work can be done at home, which allows me to be there for Mathew, and it pays well, so that's a plus."

I nodded, thinking about how challenging it would be to balance work with parenthood. It made me admire Charlie for doing it all on his own. We walked along the beach and talked for hours until Charlie finally checked his watch and realized it was way past Mathew's bedtime. Mathew protested, arguing that it was summer break, but Charlie remained firm, reminding him he needed sleep if he wanted to grow big and strong.

"But we are planning on going to the Santa Cruz beach Boardwalk tomorrow." Charlie announced. "If you don't have any plans, maybe you could join us, Samantha? And your brother is welcome, too."

I tried to think of an excuse not to go. I thought of Ron, and the fact that his health was failing. But I hadn't been to the boardwalk in years, and Mathews cute little pleading face was all it took to convince me.

"I'd love to go." I said. My heart pounded fast as I said the words, making me realize I just might be in trouble, but not the kind of trouble I wanted to avoid.

CHAPTER

The next day I woke up to find Ron and Freddy repairing the front porch. Ron looked better than he had the day before, which made me feel a whole lot better about going to the boardwalk that afternoon.

"Good morning, Samantha." He said with a smile.

"You're looking chipper today." I told him.

"I'm feeling pretty good." He answered. "Anyway, I want to get this work done while I still can. Did you have a nice time with your friends yesterday?"

I smiled, thinking of my time with Charlie and Mathew. "I had a great time. They invited me to go to the Boardwalk later on today." I looked over at Freddy, who was hammering a nail into the porch. "They invited you, too."

Freddy shrugged. "I'll think about it. If I get this all done on time."

I admired my brother's determination, at the same time, I wanted him to enjoy his summer. I decided not to push it, and just to see how the day went.

Ron cleared his throat, taking a break from sanding a piece of wood. "I want to thank you again for helping me to connect with Estelle. It was amazing to know that she's here with me. Is she here now?"

I looked over to see her sitting on a rocking chair at the far end of the porch, looking at Ron with love in her eyes.

"She's right over there." I said, gesturing toward the rocking chair she was sitting in.

He nodded. "Good. I want her here when I share the next part of our story."

We all gathered in a circle of rocking chairs, including Estelle. Ron smiled as he continued his story.

"So, about a year after I proposed to Estelle, we were married. It was a beautiful ceremony, on the beach, right over there." He gestured toward a beautiful spot down the way, where the sun seemed to glisten on the water. Estelle looked out the same way, reminiscing about the day. I understood now why this place seemed so important to her. "Estelles whole family was there, along with some mutual friends, and of course, the Martins. They were all so happy for us. We said our vows right out there on the beach."

"I told him he was the other half of my whole." Estelle whispered. "And he really was."

"The reception was at a little event center not too far from here." Ron continued. "The food was amazing, pasta and chicken. Everyone had turns wishing us well, and we danced the night away. We were big fans of *The Beatles,* so a lot of our wedding music was Beatles music. Our song was *Hey Jude,* Estelles favorite, and I sang to her as we danced that night. Everything was better than I had even envisioned. Until my dad showed up, smelling of booze and yelling obscenities at me for not inviting him. He started throwing things around, and he went after The Martins, screaming that they had no business being there. That I was his son. In the end, the police came and carried him off to jail for assault and destruction of property. As they carried him away, he claimed he'd always loved me. He said he did his best. He said he was just depressed after my mom died, that it was all so unfair. And he begged me not to let them take him to jail. I knew this was all a plea to get himself out of trouble. So, they took him, and our wedding night continued as planned."

"How long did he stay in Jail?" Freddy asked, taking a sip of his Pepsi.

Ron looked down and smiled sadly. "He hung himself in his cell the next day. I always wonder, if I had tried to get help for him, maybe things could have been different. Maybe I could have known the man he was before my mom died. But I guess I'll never know."

We all sat in silence for a beat, taking in his deep words. Finally, I knew what I wanted to say.

"It wasn't your fault. You did everything you could do for him, and it wasn't your job to save him. He was supposed to be your protector, but he failed you."

"I know you're right," Ron said with a sigh, "But he was still my father. Anyway, enough about him. I want to talk about me and Estelle. That's my happy place." Estelle leaned in to listen to him, a content smile on her face. "We had our honeymoon in Maui, and it was so beautiful. The water was so warm compared to the beaches here in California. And the people were so kind. We danced at Luau's and swam in the pool connected to our resort. We both loved the little town of Lahaina, such a charming little place to eat and shop. It seemed like a dream, only it was real, and we were happy. We bought our first house in Sacramento. I got a job as a counselor at the University, and Estelle got a job as a middle school English teacher. Our life was good, and on the right track. Only one thing was missing."

"A child." I whispered, reading his mind.

"Estelle wanted to be a mother so badly, and I wanted to be a dad. But after several years of trying, it didn't seem like it was in the cards for us. Then one day, she realized she was late, and the doctor confirmed a baby was on the way. We were ecstatic, we could hardly control our excitement. I think I started buying baby things right away, even though we didn't know if it was a boy or a girl."

Ron got up and slowly walked into the house, flinching with pain and holding his stomach as he did. In typical Ron fashion, he refused help. He went to the hall closet and retrieved what appeared to be a baby book. He handed it to me before he sat back down in his rocking chair. On the cover, it said, *'it's a girl.'*

"Eight months later, Annie Marie cunnings came into the world, all seven pounds of her. She had a head full of red hair, just like her mother and a feisty personality from the beginning."

Estelle laughed. "She sure did. I thought she would never stop crying."

I chuckled. "Estelle agrees."

Ron smiled and sat back in his rocking chair. "But as she got older, she mellowed a bit. They say when you have a child, it's like your heart is walking around outside of your body. But that doesn't even describe the emotions I felt when I held her for the first time. It's so much more than that. Being a parent really gives you a purpose, a meaning."

I turned through the pages of the book, holding it so Freddy and Estelle could see. The first five years of Annie's life were beautifully documented. Her newborn photo, every birthday, doctors' visits, including her weight and height, and the first day of kindergarten were all there. Annie posed with her kindergarten teacher, a nervous smile on her face. She looked adorable, wearing a red dress with a floral pattern and a matching red bow.

"She's adorable." I commented. "And she looks so happy."

"She was, and so were we." Ron Said. "We took her everywhere, from the very beginning. Everyone always commented on her red hair, and how beautiful it was. It was no secret where her beauty came from. She was all Estelle. Well, maybe she had my nose, but that's the only feature I could take credit for. She was a bright little thing, too. She spoke clearly by the time she was two. In nursery school, they put her with the older group of kids, and she seemed to do just fine. We were proud parents, and we loved every moment with her. The Martins came out to visit whenever they could, they became her honorary grandparents, along with Estelles' parents. Everyone loved her, she had a magnetic personality. She loved the water too. We loved going to the beach, so we brought her here to Santa Cruz all the time, and one day, I saw this place for sale. On a whim, I bought it. Estelle wasn't too happy at first. I used up most of our savings to buy this house. But it became a vacation house, and we made so many memories here. We loved sharing the place that meant so much to us with Annie. She made sandcastles and ran in the waves for hours, right out there." He gestured toward the beach, and we all looked out at it with awe. "I used to sing to her every night." He took a long breath, and quietly sang, in a scratchy voice and out of tune.

I love you in the morning,
And in the afternoon
I love you in the evening,
And underneath the moon
Skidda marink a dink a dink
Skidda marink a do
I love you.

I remembered singing that same song to Freddy when he was little. I looked over at him and realized how fast he had grown from that little boy to a young man. It really is true what they say, don't blink.

"She was always an early riser, like me, so the two of us used to get up before Estelle and make breakfast." Ron continued. "She loved pancakes, and she especially liked them when they were shaped like Mickey Mouse."

Estelle chuckled. "I could never get the ears right. Whenever I tried to make them, she told me it looked more like a rabbit."

I told Ron what Estelle said, and he laughed. "I guess I had another gift besides my spaghetti and meatballs, right dear?" Estelle agreed.

"Anyway," Ron continued, "We used to go to the park every Saturday, Just Annie and me. I wanted to give Estelle a break, and it was nice to have some father-daughter time. She loved the swings the best, and she squealed with delight when I pushed her high. She said it felt like she was flying. I used to push her on the swings, and then we would sit on the park bench. I would read the newspaper while she read the comics. Little Orphan Annie was her favorite, probably because she had the same name and red hair. She was always fascinated by it."

He paused for a moment, taking a deep breath. When I looked over at Estelle, I could tell she was tense as well.

"If this is too hard to talk about, we can always finish tomorrow." I said.

Ron shook his head. "No, I want to finish." He paused for a beat, looking out at the ocean. "I'm sure Estelle already told you I am sick. I don't have much time."

I took a deep breath and exhaled. "I know."

"So, you understand why I need to tell Annies's story?"

"I do."

"One day, just a few days after that kindergarten photo with her teacher, when she'd just turned five, I took her to the park like we did every Saturday." He continued. "I pushed her on the swings and the merry-go-round. Then she went on the slide a couple of times, and we sat on the bench to look at the newspaper, only this time, there was no little orphan Annie in the comics, so she lost interest and went off to play in the sandbox with the other kids. She seemed to be having a good time, so I continued to read the newspaper while she played. The funny thing is, I don't even remember what was in the newspaper that day. I looked up every few minutes, and she was playing happily with other children. Talking, laughing, building sandcastles together. Typical kid stuff. Then I looked up, and she was gone." Tears were forming in his eyes, but he swatted them away with his hand. "At first, I thought she went to use the restroom, but she wasn't there. I ran around, asking other parents if they had seen her, but no one had. Panic started to settle in, and I ran around screaming her name for an hour before I found a pay phone and called the police."

I looked down at my feet, feeling his pain more intensely than I had imagined. "Did they find her?"

He shook his head. "No. There was a national search for Annie. I never gave up. For years, I drove around the area of the park, thinking I might find her there, but she never was. We were on the news more times than I could count, begging whoever took her to bring her back home. I blamed myself for her disappearance. If I had only put the newspaper down. If only I hadn't taken my eyes off of her, she might still be here with me."

At that moment, both Ron and Estelle broke down in tears. And I had no idea how to comfort them.

After a few minutes, Rons sobs subsided. "I blame myself."

Estelle shook her head. "Tell him it could have happened to anyone. I did the same thing when I took her to the playground. Tell him I never blamed him. I blame whoever took our little girl."

I told Ron what Estelle said, but he just shook his head. "It didn't happen to her, it happened to me, on my watch. I had so much hope in the beginning that we would find her. But as the days and weeks and months and years drug on, it became clear that wasn't going to happen. Hope became nonexistent, even when they came up with those age progression photos. It was almost worse than death in a way. At least if they had found a body, we could have closure. We could have laid her to rest. But it was as if she disappeared into thin air. Someone said they thought they saw her in Florida one time, five years later, but that ended up being a false lead. Estelle and I still bought her presents for every birthday and Christmas, hoping she would be back someday to open them."

We all stared out at the water for a while, none of us knew the right words to say. After all, there was nothing we could say that would bring their daughter back. I wondered how their marriage could survive such a traumatic event, and Ron seemed to read my mind.

"After Annie disappeared, there was a strain on our marriage. I'm sure deep down, Estelle was angry, but she never let it show. We tried to have another baby, not to replace Annie, but to fill the deep void we felt. But age wasn't on our side, so it didn't happen. Every month was another reminder that we were childless. But we had each other, and we needed each other more than ever. So, we spent a lot of time here, in our happy place. The sound of the waves had a healing property, and although the pain of losing Annie never really went away, it became a little easier with time. I only hope whoever took her treated her with love. The thought that someone would hurt her is more than I can bear. Anyway, it takes a lot out of me to talk about this, so if you don't mind, I think I will go take a nap. I'm feeling very tired today, and everything hurts."

I helped Ron walk to his bed and pulled his covers over him. I realized how frail and weak he was, how the cancer was taking its toll. Estelle sat at his bedside, watching as he slept.

"You know," I told her, "You can cross over to the other side whenever you want. I will take care of Ron, I promise."

She shook her head, in stubborn Estelle fashion. "I think I will wait for Ron. He was the love of my life, so its only fitting that we go together. And Samantha?"

"Yes?"

"I want to thank you for everything. For being here with Ron, helping us connect, and listening to our story."

I nodded, but somehow, I wanted to do more. I went back to my room, flipped open my laptop, and googled the name Annie Marie Cunnings. Newspaper articles and T.V. news stories filled my screen, all about the missing 5-year-old and the search to bring her home. How the community rallied together to find her, to no avail. I clicked on one news segment and watched with tears in my eyes as Ron and Estelle begged for their daughter's safe return. The news segment was recorded in Annies room. The walls were pink, and her comforter was covered with beautiful pastel flowers. Estelle held one of her Teddy bears as she spoke.

"Please," She begged. "If you have information that will bring Annie home, call the number on the screen. We miss her so much, and we want her home safely."

Ron nodded. "If you know where she is, help her find her way home. There is a reward for anyone that has information. And Annie, if you are watching this, know that mommy and daddy love you so much."

Estelle and Ron both started crying after that, and the news reporter, a tall man with dark hair took over, repeating what Ron and Estelle had said, and adding that this was a missing and endangered case, and with every day that passed, there was less of a chance that Annie would be found alive. I also found an age progression photo, which showed what Annie may have looked like as a teenager. Of course, there was nothing more recent. And there was nothing that would answer the question of where she was now, or if she was still alive. I sighed as I clicked my laptop shut. Finding Annie would be like finding a needle in a haystack. Next to impossible.

CHAPTER

8

An afternoon at the Santa Cruz beach boardwalk was just what I needed to get my mind off of a very emotional morning. Charlie and Mathew showed up around noon to pick me and Freddy up. I introduced them, and Freddy actually seemed excited to go. He'd always been a daredevil and would never pass up an opportunity to ride the thrill rides. Mathew seemed excited to have an older boy around, too. He started babbling about his rock collection and how he would be starting first grade soon. Ron even came out to say goodbye before we headed out, which made me feel better about leaving him.

As we entered, a band was playing the song *Under the Boardwalk*. The smell of the ocean and delicious fried food filled the air, and people of all ages walked around, deciding which ride to go on first.

"I want to ride the Jet Copters first!" Mathew announced. It was obvious he had been here before. "And then the cave train and the Haunted Castle."

Charlie laughed. "Alright, slow down son. We have all afternoon. And I think we should ask our guests what they want to do first. That's the polite thing to do."

I laughed. "It doesn't matter to me."

Mathew looked up at his dad. "See, it doesn't matter to them. So, let's go!"

With that, he grabbed us both by the hand and led the way.

While Mathew was riding the kiddie rides, Freddy went off to do the thrill rides. I had never been a thrill seeker like my brother. Instead, I enjoyed the slower paced family style rides. Besides, this gave Charlie and I a chance to visit while Mathew was riding the rides.

"I'm glad you could come with us today." He said, meaning it.

"Thanks for inviting me." I answered. "This is just what I needed."

He nodded, waving to Mathew as he circled around on the Jet Copter. "Me, too." He turned toward me, his expression more serious. "It was exactly one year ago today that Grace died. She used to love to come here. When we were dating, we loved it here, and after Mathew was born, we would bring him, too. So, the boardwalk brings me comfort somehow. I feel like she's with me, if that makes any sense."

"It makes perfect sense." I told him.

"I just wish I could rewind time, go back to that day." He said with a sigh. "I should have gone to the store. It should be me that died that day, not her."

"Don't blame yourself." I said. "Theres no way you could have known."

"I guess not." He agreed. "It's just hard. I never thought I would be raising my son as a single dad. I pictured us doing this together."

"Life rarely goes as planned." I said. "The man we're staying with, Ron, hes the friend I was telling you about that has stage four cancer. Anyway, he's been telling me his life story, and it's been really eye opening. I think I've learned a lot from him."

"Like what?" He asked, curious.

I looked out toward the ocean, thinking about my words before I spoke. "To never take any moment for granted, because tomorrow is never promised."

"Very true." He said with a soft smile.

The rest of that afternoon was spent riding rides, playing arcade games, and eating the delicious carnival food. Charlie won a humongous teddy bear for Mathew, but Mathew insisted that I take it.

"I want to pay you back for staying with me that day." He said, with an adorable grin that was hard to say no to.

We ended our night out on the beach, listening to the band play. When they played the song *'Hey Jude,'* I thought about Ron and Estelle on their wedding day. Charlie grabbed my hand, and we danced together. I felt an electricity between us that was hard to describe, and I could tell he did too. There was an awkward pause for a moment, until we were soon interrupted by Mathew, who wanted to dance, too. So, the three of us danced and sang together until the band stopped playing. It was the best time I had ever had, and it left me wanting more.

By the time I got back to the beach house that night, Ron was already sound asleep. A half-eaten hungry man T.V. dinner sat on the table, along with a glass of water. This reminded me that his appetite was slipping too, and I wondered if he might have eaten more if I had been there with him. After all, it's always more fun to have a meal with friends. But I shook the guilty feelings away as I headed toward my room. I found Freddy in the kitchen, getting a snack of cookies and milk. I got my own midnight snack and joined him at the kitchen table.

"Thanks for taking me today." He said, meaning it.

"You're welcome. I'm just glad you're having a good time."

"I really am." He said. "I know I've been kind of a jerk lately, so thanks for putting up with me."

I dipped my cookie in the milk and took a bite. "That's what big sisters are for. I know it's not easy being a teenager. I was one once, too."

Freddy laughed. "Did you have T.V. back in those days? Or did you spend your time listening to the radio?"

I playfully poked him in the ribs. "Not that long ago. But I didn't have the latest i phone, either. The horror."

We both laughed and took another bite of our cookie along with a long gulp of milk.

"So," I continued. "I've been thinking a lot about what you said, how you want to be a medium. The thing is, everyone has their gift."

He snorted. "Ok, so what's my gift, if I even have one."

"You're an empath." I told him. Ever since we got here, you seemed to sense that Ron needed us, even before I did. You got up early to help him work on the house, even though he never asked you to do that. And you've been there for him, to listen to him when he wanted to share his story with us."

Freddy shrugged. "I guess I just felt this connection with him, that's all. And he does have an interesting story, even if it is a little depressing. Especially loosing his kid like that."

I nodded in agreement. "I wish there was a way we could find her, I mean, if she's even still alive."

Freddy dipped his cookie in his milk again, deep in thought. "Maybe there is."

My eyes widened. "Like what? How?"

"Well, when she was taken, social media and internet weren't such a big thing. But they are now. So maybe if you post something, and share it, people will share it too and it just might get back to someone who knows something. I mean, it's worth a shot."

We both finished the last gulp of our milk and clinked our glasses together.

"Little brother, I think that's a great idea."

I stayed up until the wee hours of the morning creating a virtual missing persons poster that contained all of Annies important information. It had her date of birth, hair and eye color, the date she went missing, and several pictures of her, including the age progression picture that was done over 20 years ago. I included my contact information, both phone and e mail. And I gave it one final look before I sent it out into the universe of Facebook, twitter and Instagram. I just hoped as I fell asleep that night that someone would see it and have answers about what happened to Annie. And I hoped it was soon, because time wasn't on our side.

CHAPTER

9

I woke up the next day to a huge teddy bear sitting in the corner, and it seemed to be staring at me, waiting for me to wake up. I laughed, remembering Mathew's cute little face when he gave it to me. I also wondered where on earth I was going to put it when I got back home. But right now, I had more important matters to tend to. I grabbed my phone to check if there were any bites on social media about Annie. There was nothing, so I slipped out of bed, got dressed and showered, and headed out to grab a cup of coffee. Since everyone was still sleeping, I went out for my typical morning walk, sipping my coffee as I strolled along the beach, the waves tickling my ankles as I walked along. The crisp morning air was refreshing, and a blanket of fog hovered over me, making it hard to see far ahead. But I knew it would lift by mid-afternoon. My phone buzzed in my pocket, and when I pulled it out, I saw that it was my aunt Michelle calling. She was my mom's younger sister, and we had always been close. I was happy to hear her voice.

"Hello, Aunt Michelle."

"Hello, Neice. How are you? It's been a minute. I saw your post on Facebook. Who is this missing girl and why are you trying to find her?"

"It's a long story." I told her.

"I have time."

"Well, the old man who owns the beach house Freddy and I are staying at, it turns out he's dying. Cancer. And I have talked to his dead wife, who wants me to stay with him until the end."

Michelle was one of the few people I could freely talk to about my ability to talk to dead people. She'd never judged me or made me feel different.

"Wow, that's heavy." She said.

"Tell me about it. Anyway, he's been telling me his life story. How he met his wife when they were kids, and they fell in love. They really are like one of those supercouples you read about in romance novels. And that little girl is their daughter who disappeared over 50 years ago."

She paused as she let this soak in. "Do you think she's still alive?"

I shrugged. "It's hard to tell, but it was worth a shot."

"Well, if anyone can find her, it would be you."

"Thanks."

"So, how is it going with Freddy?" She asked with a chuckle. "I hear he's really asserting his autonomy lately."

"He actually hasn't been too bad." I said. "He and Ron seem to get along. He's been helping him fix up the house. And he went to the Boardwalk with me and some friends yesterday."

"You have friends in Santa Cruz? You've only been there a few days."

"I know." I said. "Its just some guy and his son."

"Just some guy, huh?"

"Yeah. His name is Charlie."

"Well, from the tone of your voice, I don't think he's just some guy. You like him, don't you?"

I sighed. "Maybe. Just a little. But it's complicated. Anyway, I invited him over this afternoon to swim and barbeque. Freddy and Ron worked hard to get the pool up and running."

I could hear her take a deep breath. "Okay, well I think I should come check this guy out, make sure he's not a criminal. Besides, the twins are driving me crazy. It would be nice to get them out of the house."

Miles and Millie were Michelles' 4-year-old twins, and their dad was away on business often, leaving her to tend to two very active preschoolers on her own. I hadn't seen my aunt or my younger cousins in months, so the thought of spending time with them brought a smile to my face.

"You really want to come to Santa Cruz?"

"Is that an invite?" she asked, with a pleading tone in her voice.

I smiled, relieved to have someone around who really understood me. Someone who accepted me for me. "Yes, it's an invite. Dinner is at 5."

"I will be there with bells on."

I went to the nearby store to get everything I would need for our barbeque that afternoon. Hamburgers, hot dogs, and chicken, too. I got sides of mashed potatoes, mac and cheese, and corn on the cob. I also got a tank of propane for the grill, which probably hadn't been used in years. So, I cleaned it and tested it out. I was relieved when it worked perfectly. Now the only thing missing were the guests. Charlie and Mathew showed up around 4, both looking handsome in their matching swim trunks and swim shirts. Ron and Freddy waited out on the porch and greeted them with a smile. Soon after that, my aunt Michelle showed up, with Miles and Millie in tow, full of energy as ever. I introduced everyone and the kids all raced toward the pool.

"I'm gonna do a cannon ball!" Miles squealed at the top of his lungs.

"Well, I'm gonna do a belly flop first!" Millie said, crossing her arms over her chest.

"My dad won't let me swim without a life vest in the ocean." Mathew said, disappointed. "But I can show you all my swim skills in the pool. I took swim classes, and I was a master dolphin."

"I can't wait to see what you can do." I told him.

"I hope you don't mind that I brought squirt guns." Charlie said. "They were on sale at the dollar store, and Mathew insisted."

"That sounds like fun." I said, smiling at them both.

The classic rock station played on the radio as we all swam that afternoon, singing and laughing. Ron even joined us for a while, noting that he hadn't been in the pool for over five years. I was relieved to see that he was having such a good day.

"It's about time." Mathew announced, as he squirted him with his squirt gun. Ron just laughed, grabbing a squirt gun of his own and squirting him back. Before we knew it, we were all in a full-blown squirt gun battle. And it didn't matter who won, because we were all having that much fun.

Freddy helped with the grill that afternoon, and we all enjoyed a meal together, laughing and talking as we ate. Like the protective aunt she was, Michelle asked Charlie all sorts of questions about his job, his life, and what he liked to do with his free time. Of course, most of his answers revolved around Mathew.

After Mathew and Charlie went home that night, Aunt Michelle and I sat out on the front porch, looking out at the ocean while her kids played nearby in the sand.

"Charlie seems nice." She said. "And Mathew is adorable."

I nodded in agreement. "I've enjoyed spending time with them."

Her expression turned more serious. "I just want you to be careful. If you do end up in a relationship with this guy, there's more than one person involved."

"I realize that." I told her. "And we're just friends, anyway."

She gave me the side eye. "I saw how you look at each other." She tried to mimic the way we look at each other, by playfully batting her eyelashes, making me laugh.

"I wouldn't go that far. He's just a nice guy. Like I said, we're just friends."

"Maybe you are. Or maybe its just too soon to tell." She said.

"Maybe." I agreed.

She lowered her voice. "Ron is such a sweet man. It's hard to believe he's dying. He seemed so full of life today."

"He has good days and bad days." I told her. "But it won't be long before the bad days outnumber the good." I shuddered at the thought of Ron lying in his bed, unable to move.

"I know this must be a lot for you." She said, her voice full of compassion. "Just make sure you take care of yourself too, ok?"

I nodded. "I will."

She put her arm around me, pulling me into a hug. "I love you, niece."

I didn't know who needed that hug more, but I hugged her tight, taking in the familiar scent of her Chanel perfume. "I love you, too, aunt."

I fell asleep that night content, happy it had been such a good day with family and friends. At the same time, I was afraid of what might happen in the days ahead.

CHAPTER

The next few days were pretty much the same, with no change in Ron's condition, which was a good thing, and no word on Annie, which was disappointing. Charlie and I spent a lot of time together, at the beach with Mathew, and one night he invited me over for dinner at his place. He said he wanted to cook for me and have dinner together after Mathew was in bed. I was excited and nervous about time alone with him, Mathew had always been around as a sort of buffer between us, and I was afraid of what might happen when that buffer was gone.

When I arrived at his beach house, just a short walk down the beach from where I was staying, Mathew tackled me with a hug, looking adorable as always in his race car pajamas. His hair was damp and smelled like watermelon.

"Come on, Samantha, I want to show you my rock collection!" he said, grabbing my hand and leading me to his room. On the far wall was a display case with hundreds of rocks. "You see, that's an igneous rock." He pointed to an odd-shaped rock with holes in it. "And that one is a Metamorphic rock, that is a Basalt rock, and that one is Sedimentary."

"Wow, you really know your rocks." I said, impressed.

Charlie shrugged. "He's always been fascinated by rocks. Pretty soon I'll have to get a bigger display case. Anyway, son, remember what we talked about. I want you to brush your teeth and get ready for bed."

"Aww, do I have to?" Mathew pleaded.

"Yes, you do." Charlie said, remaining firm.

Mathews eyes lit up, and I could tell he had another idea to stall bedtime. "Can Samantha read me a bedtime story tonight?"

Charlie looked at me, with an apologetic smile. "Only if she wants to."

I beamed. "I would love to."

After I had read *Goodnight Moon* 3 times, Mathew was out within minutes, snoring quietly as his head rested on my shoulder.

Charlie and I sat out on his front porch, in comfortable silence until he got up and carried out two wine glasses and a bottle of pinot noir.

"Would you like some?"

I nodded. "Sure. Pinot noir has always been my favorite."

"I know, I mean I remember you saying something about that."

He fumbled with the wine opener until I heard a pop, and he poured each of us a half glass of wine. He handed me one and took a sip from the other. I took a sip out of my own glass, savoring the smooth flavor as it went down.

"Thanks for coming over tonight." He said, his voice soft.

"Thanks for inviting me."

"Well, Mathew has been dying to show you his rock collection." He took another sip of his wine, choosing his words carefully. "And I have my own selfish reasons for inviting you over tonight."

I gulped, feeling my heart drum in my chest. "Like what?"

"Like, I really enjoy spending time with you."

I could feel the heat rise in my cheeks. "I enjoy spending time with you, too."

He beamed. "Good. Well, you're in for a treat tonight. I have steak, baked potatoes, and a nice Caesar salad. I hope that's ok."

"That sounds perfect." I said.

"Well, its nice to have an adult to eat with." Charlie laughed. "All Mathew ever wants is chicken fingers."

"He ate corn and a hot dog at my place the other day." I pointed out.

"True. And I do try to get him to eat other things."

I smiled. "No judgement here. Freddy went through a phase where he lived on peanut butter and jelly for like six months."

We both laughed, lightening the mood.

"So, when do you go back to work?" He asked, swirling the wine in his glass.

"In four more weeks." I answered. "Unless Ron needs me longer."

"Well, I admire what you do." He said, meaning it. "I feel like I can barely control one 5-and-a-half-year-old, I can't imagine 24 of them."

"Its challenging but rewarding for sure." I said. "I can't imagine doing something else."

"Its good you found your calling." He said. "Sometimes I feel like I still don't know what I want to do. I mean, my job with the insurance company gives me a paycheck, but I wonder if there's more out there, you know?"

I nodded. "I know exactly what you mean."

We continued our conversation, losing track of time. I was so relaxed, maybe from the wine or the company that I didn't notice that he was scooting closer to me until I felt his arm around my waist. I felt myself relax, scooting closer to him. Tingles surged through me as he gently rubbed my back. He leaned in closer, his face almost touching mine.

"To much?" He whispered, running his fingers through my hair. "Because I want to kiss you so bad right now."

I leaned in, pressing my lips against his, giving him the answer he wanted. He kissed me gently at first, quickly becoming more urgent. Then he kissed my neck and my cheek before moving back to my lips. My pulse raced and I felt something I had never felt before. I mean, I had kissed and been kissed, but nothing compared to this. When he finally pulled away, we were both breathless.

"Wow." He whispered. "That was amazing."

I nodded, still trembling and unable to find the words.

He took my hand in his, making circles with his thumb, making my heart pound even harder, if that was even possible. "Well, I guess I should start dinner." He said, still trying to catch his breath. "To be continued?"

I nodded. "To be continued."

He went to the kitchen to start dinner. I had offered to help, but he refused, saying that I was the guest tonight and he wanted me to relax. So, I sat on the rocking chair, sipping my wine and looking out at the beach. It wasn't long before I noticed the silhouette of a woman walking along the beach in the dark. And it wasn't just any woman, she had that glow that I recognized as being a spirit. And she was wearing a yellow sundress. I started to hyperventilate when I realized who that spirit was.

I peeked through the window and saw that Charlie was still busy preparing dinner, so I tiptoed out to the beach to get a closer look. She seemed to walk faster, as if she was trying to get away from me.

"Grace?" I called. "Is that you?"

She turned around slowly, and she seemed surprised that I knew her name.

"You can see me?" she asked in disbelief.

I nodded. "My name is Samantha. I'm a medium. I can speak to people who have passed away. And I can help them cross over."

"That's amazing." She said. "Because I have been walking around all this time, trying to find someone who could understand me."

"Well, you found her." I said, recalling what had taken place on the porch just minutes before. I felt awkward when I thought about Grace watching me kiss her husband. "So, um, exactly how long have you been watching?"

"Long enough." She said.

I took a deep breath. "Sorry about that. I mean, if I had known you were there I wouldn't have, we wouldn't have........."

She held up her hand as if to swipe away my words. "Please, don't apologize. I'm the one who's intruding. I'm the one who shouldn't be here."

"Well, there's a reason you're still here." I said. "Usually when spirits stay here on earth, it's because they have some sort of unfinished business. And its my job to help you figure out what that is so you can cross over."

She paused for a beat, thinking about my words. "I think I know what that is."

I thought to myself that was easy. Most spirits needed time to think about what their unfinished business was.

"I want to know that Charlie is happy." She said. "I don't know if he told you this, but after I died, he was in a deep depression. He didn't eat, he barely slept. It was hard for me to watch. And that day you found Mathew on the beach, he had taken some sleeping pills and fallen asleep. So, Mathew wondered off, and if you hadn't found him, well, I hate to think of what might have happened. So, I want to thank you for that."

"Of course, you're more than welcome." I said, my voice soft.

"Anyway," She continued, "I've been watching the three of you, and I can tell you make Charlie and Mathew very happy. I guess, what I want is to know that you'll be there for them when I can't? Fill in the missing space where I used to be?"

I gulped. "You want me to replace you?"

"Not replace me exactly." She said. "But I want you to be their person. I want you to light up their days and be the mother to Mathew that he desperately needs. I know that's a lot to ask, but I think that's what I need to move on."

"I'm not sure if I can do that." I whispered.

"I need you to try." She said before she disappeared.

"Samantha?" Charlie called as he walked toward the beach. "What are you doing out here?" He looked around. "Were you talking to someone?"

I turned toward him, my heart thumping in my chest. "No. I mean I was. I went for a walk just to stretch my legs. My phone rang, so I answered it, but it was only spam, so I hung up."

He smiled, relieved. "Good, because I came out to offer you a refill of wine, and when you were gone, I thought maybe you left. I thought maybe I scared you away."

I smiled. "Not at all."

"Good." He said, reaching for my hand. "Because I really want to see where this could go."

"Me, too." I said, taking his hand as we walked back toward the house together.

Charlie prepared a gourmet meal, the steak was cooked perfectly, the salad was fresh, the potatoes were delicious. But I couldn't stop thinking about my encounter with Grace. What she was asking seemed almost impossible. There was no way I could take her place. And although I had thought about having kids in the very distant future, and Mathew was adorable, I didn't feel prepared to be a mother. Charlie seemed to sense that I was a million miles away, and he brought me back to earth.

"Is everything okay? You seem kind of distant." He said, reaching across the table to touch my hand.

"I'm fine." I answered. "I just have a lot on my mind."

His expression was one of disbelief. "I just hope I wasn't too forward earlier. I want you to know that's usually not like me. And I know we haven't known each other that long, but there's just something about you. And Mathew talks about you all the time, too. And that's saying a lot, because he doesn't just bond with anyone."

"He's a wonderful little boy." I said. "You're doing a fantastic job with him."

"Thank you." He said, taking another sip of his wine. "That means a lot, coming from an educator."

"I'm just being honest."

"I do my best." He said quietly. "But I wonder sometimes if its good enough."

"Don't doubt yourself." I told him. "You're a great dad."

He was quiet for a moment, taking a bite of his potato, followed by another a sip of wine. "Can I ask you something, Samantha?"

"Sure." I said, taking another sip of my own wine.

"Does the fact that I have a child scare you away? I mean, I know it's probably not what most women your age are looking for. Most are still in the stage where they want to go out and party all the time. My evenings are mostly filled with bath time and bedtime stories. Not exactly exciting, but I wouldn't change it for the world."

I looked him in the eyes and placed my hand on his. "Tonight, was perfect, just the three of us."

"I'm glad you feel that way." He said. "Because I can see a lot more nights like that in the future."

"I can too." I agreed.

He seemed pleased with my answer, and he pulled my chair closer to his, and kissed me, only this time he didn't pause to ask my permission. I kissed him back, feeling a surge of something that can only be described as euphoria. And that feeling continued as we walked inside and continued to make out on the couch. His hands were warm as he started to unbutton my shirt. My eyes darted toward Mathew's bedroom door, and Charlie seemed to read my mind. We both didn't want to take any chances of Mathew coming out and finding us. He took my hand and led me to his room, locking the door behind us. Then we continued to undress each other. I pulled his shirt over his head, revealing his muscular build that made my body tingle with excitement. He finished unbuttoning my shirt and tossed it on the floor beside us. Then his hands reached around my back where he fumbled until he finally unfastened my bra. He kissed both of my breasts as I unsnapped his jeans, then he pulled his jeans off and tossed them on the floor, too, revealing his teal boxers. He gently pulled me on top of him. His excitement was evident as he pressed his body against mine. I kissed his chest, his neck and worked my way back to his lips. He slipped my skirt off and gently ran his fingers through my hair, down my neck, over my breasts, and my stomach until his fingers lingered on the lace edge of my panties, making me moan with excitement. His touch was unlike anything I had ever felt before. He looked me in the eyes, silently asking for permission. And I wanted to give it to him, probably more than I had ever wanted anything. But suddenly, Graces words started echoing in my mind. *Fill in the missing space where I used to be. Be the Mother Mathew so desperately needs.* How would I ever be able to fill her shoes? This was all too much pressure. Besides, what if I told Charlie the truth about my ability to talk to dead people? Would he believe me? Or would he think I was crazy and run for the hills, just like every other guy I dated. I pulled away, kissing him one more time.

He looked at me, confused. "Is everything alright?"

I scrambled to find my clothes. "I'm sorry, Charlie. I can't do this. Not tonight."

"Why not? Did I do something wrong? Or say something wrong? Whatever it is we can talk about it."

I continued to get dressed, slipping into my shirt and buttoning it up before I had a chance to change my mind. "No, you did everything right." I assured him. "It's not you, it's me. And it's complicated."

He took my chin in his hand, turning my head toward him. His eyes were full of worry and desperation. "Please, just talk to me."

I found my sandals and slipped them on. "I can't. Not right now. I'm sorry, but I have to go."

He shook his head, his eyes moist with tears. "Please, stay."

I put my hand on his, feeling tears well up in my own eyes. "I wish I could, but I can't."

I grabbed my purse and walked out the door, without another word. And I knew it was going to be a long night.

CHAPTER

11

I spent most of that night tossing and turning, thoughts about that night raced through my head. My feelings for Charlie were stronger than anything I had ever felt. I wanted to tell him the truth about my abilities, and also the fact that I had spoken with Grace. But how would he react? There was no way to tell. We had never even talked about life after death, or his feelings on the subject. This was one of those times I wished I was born just like everyone else. Then I never would have known Grace was hanging around, or that she wanted me to be her replacement.

When morning finally came, I tiptoed out to the kitchen where I found Ron sipping his coffee and reading the paper. He looked up at me and smiled.

"Good morning."

"Good morning." I said as I walked over to the coffee pot and poured myself a cup.

He seemed to read that I was a little off, and he sat his paper down. "Is everything alright, Samantha?"

I nodded. "Sure. Everything is fine. I should be asking you that. How are you feeling?"

He shrugged. "So, so. I've felt better, but I've also felt worse, so that's a good thing."

"Good." I said. "I hope you're being honest with me. And please let me know if you want to get a doctor involved. Maybe they can help you with your pain."

He shook his head. "I've seen more doctors than I can count, and every one of them just made me feel worse. No more treatments, and no more needles. I want to go out on my own terms."

I admired his determination, and if I had been in the same place, I wondered what I would do.

"Anyway," He continued. "I want to hear about your date last night. Charlie seems like a really nice fellow."

Hearing Charlie's name made my pulse quicken. "Yes, he is. And we had a really great night. We put Mathew to bed and had a nice dinner. We really enjoy each other's company. But it's also complicated."

"Complicated how?"

"I sighed. "I'm not sure I'm ready to talk about it."

He nodded. "Fair enough. But when you're ready, just let me know. I'm a good listener, that's one thing I can still do. Don't wait too long, though, because I might not be around." He said with a chuckle.

I smiled. "I won't."

He looked around the room. "Is Estelle here today?"

I saw her sitting in a chair in the corner, looking out the window. She looked toward us when she heard her name.

"She's right over there." I gestured toward the chair where she was sitting.

Ron beamed. "Good morning sweetheart."

"Good morning." She answered.

My heart filled with joy watching the two of them communicate and I admired their love that had even survived death. That was the kind of love I wanted someday, but it seemed almost impossible.

"Did I ever tell you Estelle was a really good dancer?" Ron asked, bringing me back to the present. "She even ran her own dance company for a while after Annie disappeared. I think it gave her something positive to focus on, to keep her mind busy so she wouldn't spend every minute thinking about Annie. She enrolled us in some dance classes, too. I fought her at first, but it was actually fun, and we met some other couples with similar interests. We even kept in touch with some of them for years. One couple in particular, the Mizner's became our cruise partners. Every summer, we went on a different cruise together. To Mexico, Alaska, Hawaii. And we even went on a world cruise together." He smiled, lightly. "Those were some good times."

Estelle nodded in agreement, "Yes, they were. Especially when you'd had too much to drink, and you tried to sing karaoke. And you actually thought you were a good singer."

I laughed, and repeated what Estelle had told me.

"Hey, I take offence to that!" Ron said with a chuckle. "People said I sound just like Paul McCartney."

Estelle laughed. "Not quite, but when you sang *Hey Jude* to me, it did make me think of our wedding day."

I told Ron what Estelle had said, and they both seemed lost in their thoughts as they reminisced about that day. I could picture it myself, just as I had been there. But my thought was interrupted when there was a knock at the door.

"I wonder who that could be." Ron Said. "I don't get many visitors these days."

I had a feeling I knew who it was, and when I got up to answer the door, I was right. Charlie and Mathew both stood there, one looking as happy as ever, and one seemed depressed, looking down toward the ground.

"Samantha, I found a new rock!" Mathew exclaimed. "This one has some pink in it." He held out his palm to reveal a beautifully colored rock.

"Wow." I said. "I think that is one of the most unique rocks in your collection." I looked over at Charlie, but it was hard to read his expression. It was somewhere between hurt and confusion, and I knew exactly why.

"Mathew insisted we stop by so he could show you his rock." He said, with a slight smile on his face. "I was hoping we could go for a walk and talk?"

I nodded and went to get my sweater. The mornings on the beach were always a little chilly.

We walked along the beach in silence for a while, watching Mathew throw some rocks into the waves, and save others for his collection. I was thinking about what I could say to break the tension between us when Charlie finally spoke.

"Just be honest with me, did I do something wrong?"

"No." I said without hesitation. "Like I said, it isn't you, it's me."

"Can you at least try to explain what happened?" He pleaded. "I mean, I thought we were having a great night, and all of the sudden, it was like something changed. And I noticed you were acting different after you went for a walk on the beach."

I sighed. "I want to explain it to you, I really do, but it's not that simple."

He nodded. "I think I get it."

I narrowed my eyes. "You do?"

"Yah." He said. "You're scared. Scared of commitment, scared of getting hurt, and scared to take a chance. I feel the same way." He reached over to take my hand. "But I think I can overcome that fear because you're worth it."

I felt my face turn red at the sincerity of his words. "I think you're worth it, too. But there's more to it than that."

"Like what?" He asked. But before I could answer, Mathew came up behind us and squirted us both with his squirt gun, giggling with his adorable little boy giggle.

"Got you good!"

Charlie laughed and pulled two squirt guns out of his own pocket, handing one to me.

"You're gonna pay for that!" He said. And suddenly, nothing else mattered but the three of us and our squirt gun war. We ran along the beach, squirting each other, but it didn't seem to matter who won. We were all having so much fun. After our battle was over, Charlie and I sat on a warm spot on the beach to dry off while Mathew made sandcastles in the distance.

"So, do you think we could just start over?" He asked. "I've really enjoyed spending time with you. I don't want things to be strange or awkward between us."

"Me neither." I said, quietly. "I just wish it was that simple."

"It can be." He said with so much confidence I almost believed him.

I thought about his words for a moment, as a lump formed in my throat. "Can I ask you something? You have to promise to answer honestly."

He gently took my hand in his, making my pulse quicken again. "Anything."

"What do you think happens to someone when they die?"

He seemed surprised at my question, but he answered it quickly. "I think it's just like when you go to sleep."

"Really?" I said with a crack in my voice. "You don't thing there's more to it?"

He shook his head. "Nope. I've always been a realist, I guess. If I can't see it or feel it, I don't believe it's real. I mean, that would be strange if there were dead people walking around. And heaven? I think that's just a story we tell ourselves so we can feel better about death."

I took a deep breath, taking in his words, which stung just as if he had slapped me. "That's really how you feel?"

He nodded. "Yes, it is. And don't even let me get started on those people who claim they can speak to dead people. Mediums, or whatever you want to call them. They are all just frauds that just want to steal money from people."

All of a sudden, I felt dizzy, I stood up, trying to find my balance. It was hard to breathe, and I needed to get as far away from him as possible. "I need to go."

Charlie looked confused. "What happened, did I say something wrong? You asked me to be honest."

"And I'm glad you were." I told him. "Tell Mathew I said goodbye."

I turned around and walked back toward the beach house without looking back.

CHAPTER

12

The rest of that day and night were like a blur. I made sandwiches for lunch and chicken with pasta for dinner, which was a good thing because it gave me something to focus on besides Charlie. Freddy and Ron worked around the house, but Ron needed to rest more often than normal, and spent most of his time in bed. Although he would never admit it, I could tell he was in pain. But after dinner, we all sat out on the front porch, looking out at the water. It was getting colder outside, so I wrapped a blanket around Rons shoulders, and we all listened as he finished his story about Estelle.

"Estelle was always full of life, a ball full of energy." He chuckled. "She'd never had anything more serious than a cold in her life, and everyone admired her tenacity. She really was a force to be reckoned with, and I felt so lucky she was mine. Even after she'd retired from teaching, she still went back as a substitute teacher because she loved the kids that much. She received teacher of the year awards more times than I can count, and she mentored new teachers through a program at the university." His eyes twinkled as he talked about the love of his life. "She really was something special."

Estelle sat near us on a bench, and she flicked her hand in the air. "I wasn't that special." She chuckled. "But tell Ron he can continue."

I laughed. "Estelle says you can continue, I think she likes all the praise." I whispered.

"She deserves it." Ron said. "Anyway, she stayed active until that day." His face turned from a smile to a frown. "We went to the grocery store that morning. We got everything for my famous spaghetti and meatballs, because she was tired, and I wanted to make dinner. I bought her a bouquet of her favorite flowers, but I made the mistake of leaving the price tag on, so we got in a tiff about spending money on frivolous things. I told her it was only a kind gesture, and it shouldn't matter how much the flowers cost because she was worth every penny. In the end, we agreed to disagree, and she went out to tend her garden while I started dinner. When dinner was almost finished, I went to check on her." His voice cracked with emotion. "I found her collapsed on the ground. She had a pulse, but it was weak. I called the paramedics, and I started CPR until they arrived. When they came to take over, I could tell it wasn't good. I sat beside her in the ambulance, begging her to stay with me. Promising I would be a better husband, a better man if only she would fight to stay with me."

Estelle came and put a hand on his shoulder. "Tell him he was the best husband a girl could ask for. It was just my time."

I repeated what she'd said, and Ron smiled a sad smile. "The rest of that night was a blur. The doctors said words like brain aneurism, told me there was nothing I could have done. They said she most likely didn't feel any pain, but that didn't bring my Estelle back." Tears trailed down his cheek. "I miss her so much."

Estelle stroked his hair lovingly. "I'm still here, darling."

Ron reached up to touch his hair, I could tell he felt something. Estelle sat her hand on his, and again, I was touched by the deep love these two shared.

CHAPTER

13

The next few days were much the same, except for one noticeable difference. Ron was spending more and more time in bed, which meant time was not on our side. I started to have doubts about why I was there, what my role was, and if I could really make a difference at this point. I had always had so much confidence in my abilities and my gift to help people, but that seemed to be shrinking all the time. And then, out of the blue, there was a ding on my phone and a notification of a new Facebook post on my page dedicated to finding Annie. I quickly scrolled and checked my messages. And there was one by Pamela George.

> Hello, Samantha
>
> My name is Pam George, but that wasn't the name I was born with. I believe I am Annie Cunnings and I saw your post on Facebook. I was adopted by a family when I was 5 years old, or at least that was what I was led to believe. I was told my family could not take care of me, so they chose a new family who could provide for me. I believed this, since my dad Ron had recently lost his job. So, I went with them

willingly when I was approached at the park that day, a mistake I still regret.

The Georges were a wonderful family that showed me so much love, but I always knew something was missing. After I saw your post on Facebook, I knew what that missing piece was. I still have memories of my birth parents, and I hope to connect with them soon. After I saw your post I confronted my adoptive mother, Valerie who was on her death bed from a bacterial infection and has since passed away. She admitted that her and my father had wanted a child for many years and my father Adam who died three years ago had been watching me every Saturday at the park. He saw an opportunity when Ron was looking at the paper, and he approached me, explaining that he was my new father, since Ron could no longer care for me. He brought me home to Valerie, and I like to believe I filled their home with happiness and love. They were not horrible people; they were just desperate to raise a child. They have both passed on now, but I would love a chance to connect with my biological parents. This is something I think about every day, and I hope you can help me connect with them before it is too late. Thank you for posting this and hope to connect soon.

Pamela George

I was left frozen, unsure of what to do. But then, I knew what I needed to do next. I pushed the reply button and sent a message to Pam George, AKA Annie Cunnings. And this was the most important message I had ever sent.

After I wrote the message, I took a walk along the beach while sipping my coffee. It began to sink in that I actually might be able to reunite Ron with his long-lost daughter, and that was a really good feeling. But I also felt sad because I wished they could have more time. As I was thinking about all of this, I suddenly got the feeling that someone was watching me, and I turned around to see Grace's spirit following me, her yellow sundress blowing in the wind.

"Please talk to me." She said, her voice low.

"There isn't much to talk about." I said, matter of fact. "It isn't going to work out with Charlie and me. It never was."

"How do you know?" She pleaded.

"Because I just know." I told her. "This is just like every other relationship I have had. As soon as they find out I'm a medium, they treat me like some sort of freak, a crazy person. I already know what he thinks about people like me."

"Just give him a chance." She said. "He'll come around. "You have to tell him."

I took a deep breath, choosing my words carefully. "Listen, Grace, you seem like a really nice person, or spirit, and I want to help you cross over to the other side. But what you're asking is too much. You're asking me to put my own heart on the line, and I'm not willing to do that. So, I'm sorry, but I can't help you."

She looked down at the ground, defeated. "Isn't that what love is all about? You put your heart on the line just for that chance, and when it happens, it's like magic. Theres really no way to describe it until you feel it. You and Charlie are meant to be together; I can tell. And Mathew needs you."

"Honestly, Grace, I have a lot going on right now." I said, maintaining my patience. "I'm taking care of a very sick man and my younger brother. So, I don't have the time or energy to focus on a relationship. Charlie is a great guy, and I'm sure he will find someone special, but that someone special isn't me."

With those words, I turned around and continued walking without looking back.

⚜

The hours went by slowly while I waited for Pam, AKA Annie, to arrive. I explained to her that her dad didn't have much time left, if she wanted to see him, she needed to hurry. Ron wouldn't get out of bed and remained asleep most of the day. When I spoke to him, his eyes fluttered open and shut again just as fast. I hoped he could hold on just a little bit longer. Long enough to spend time with his long-lost daughter. I explained to Freddy what had happened, and he seemed just as excited as I was to see Ron reunite with his daughter. But also concerned that he might not make it.

"I've never seen him so shut down." He said. "He didn't even wake up when we were supposed to work around the house, and he is always excited to do that. And He didn't even eat a bite of his breakfast."

"I know." I said. "I think his body is just tired of fighting. All of his organs are shutting down. He might not make it to meet Annie after all of these years."

Freddy looked down at the ground, contemplating what I had just said. "Should we at least tell him then? So, he knows she is still alive?"

I shook my head. "No. I want him to see it himself. And don't ask me how, but I believe he will."

Freddy thought about my words for a moment. "Then I believe it too."

I smiled. "You do?"

"I do." He said. "You always know these things. And most of the time, you're right."

I put an arm around my brother, grateful to have someone who believed in me.

"Thanks, brother."

"You're welcome, sister."

We both checked on Ron, who grew weaker by the minute. He did wake up long enough to eat some vegetable soup, but his hands were shaky, so I fed him. Normally Ron would be too stubborn to accept that type of care, but he opened his mouth willingly as I put the spoon in his mouth.

"Thank you for everything, Samantha." He said in a hoarse voice. "For being here, for listening to my story, and just for your company."

"You're more than welcome." I told him.

He put his hand on mine, but it felt ice cold. "I want you to know all of my bank information is in the file cabinet in my little office. I already called the bank and told them I wanted you to have whatever is left in the account, as well as this house. I just hope you and Freddy enjoy it as much as Estelle and I did. There are just a few papers I need you to fill out. Everything I own is debt free, so you won't have to worry about any of that."

I felt a lump in my throat. "You don't have to do that."

He shrugged. "Who else am I going to give it to? My family is long gone, most of my friends have passed away, and my only daughter is most likely dead. You and Freddy are the closest thing I have to family."

I nodded. "Thank you. But there is something you should know." His eyes fluttered shut, and just as quickly as he woke up, he was asleep again. "Ron. Ron?" I called, my voice full of worry. But there was no answer.

The minutes ticked on as we waited for Annies's arrival. And finally, there was a knock on the door. I threw the door open to see a much older, but unmistakable Annie. And with her was a young woman, holding a newborn baby. They all had beautiful red hair.

"I made it here as fast as I could." She said, out of breath. "This is my daughter Angela, and her baby girl, Kaitlyn."

My eyes widened as I took in the beauty of it all. Not only would Ron be meeting his daughter, but his granddaughter and great-granddaughter as well. This was truly a magical moment. That is, if he woke up long enough to meet them. As I spoke, Freddy came walking out of Rons room, shaking his head. And tears were puddled up in his eyes.

"I can't get him to wake up, Samantha. I think it's too late."

I wrapped my brother in a hug, just like I used to do when he was younger, and he'd had a bad dream.

"It can't be." I looked at Annie and Angela and could see the disappointment on their faces.

"I tried to get here as fast as I could." Annie said. "I was even pulled over for speeding, but when I explained to the officer what I was doing, he actually followed me the rest of the way to make sure I was safe. So can I at least see him?"

I nodded. "Of course. Follow me." I led the three of them into Rons room, where he lay motionless. Annie rushed to his side and took his hand in hers.

"He's so cold."

"I know." I said. "He's been that way the last few days. "I've tried hand warmers, heated blankets. Everything."

She nodded. "Thank you for taking such good care of him. I just wish I got here a little sooner."

I was not willing to accept that this was the end. That after all of this, he would never get to meet his daughter, granddaughter, and great granddaughter. Estelle sat on the other side of his bed, holding his hand. And there were tears of joy in her eyes.

"He's still alive, Samantha. And I'm here too. Thank you for bringing Annie home." She looked at Angela and baby Kaitlyn, her eyes full of love. "And my granddaughter and great-granddaughter. This is really a miracle."

"What should I do?" I whispered, under my breath.

Estelle nodded, sure of her words. "Have Annie talk to him."

I nodded. "I think you should talk to your dad. I don't know how you feel about life after death, but I believe he can hear you."

She nodded, and turned to Ron, his hand in her hand. Estelle looked on with happy tears in her eyes. "Hi, daddy, It's me, Annie. I'm here with my beautiful daughter Angela and her baby girl Kaitlyn." She chuckled. "That's right, you old goat, you have a great-granddaughter. Can you believe it?" She shook her head, tears falling down her cheek. "I just want you to know I am so sorry for wandering off that day. You told me about stranger danger, and I should have listened to you. But Adam seemed like such a kind man. I want you to know they never hurt me. I was loved. They were just desperate to raise a child, and although it doesn't make it right to take me the way they did, they weren't horrible people. They have both died now, but I want you to know I remember you. I remember the pancakes on Saturday morning, reading the comics, especially Litte Orphan Annie. And playing at the park. I remember the song you used to sing to me at bedtime." She sang the song in a beautiful voice that made me think she should be a singer.

I love you in the morning,
And in the afternoon
I love you in the evening,
And underneath the moon.
Shidda marink a dink a dink
Skidda marink a do
I love you."

With those words, she laid her head on her father's chest and sobbed. Tears filled my eyes too as I took in the emotion of it all. But then, something miraculous happened. Rons eyes fluttered open, and he looked right at his daughter. He recognized her immediately.

"Annie?"

Annie lifted her head and looked him in the eyes.

"Yes, daddy, its me."

"You're alive." He said in a weak voice.

"Alive and well." She said with a smile. "And I brought my daughter Angela and her baby Kaitlyn."

He looked at the two of them, with love in his eyes. Angela brought the baby closer, so he could see her. Ron reached his hand up and baby Kaitlyn wrapped her tiny fingers around his.

"Samantha, look at this. I have a great-granddaughter!" He said.

"I know." I said, my voice cracking with emotion. Freddy stood behind us, watching it all, and I could tell he was a little emotional himself.

Annie reached into her pocket and pulled out her phone. "Do you mind taking a few pictures of us?"

I nodded, and reached for her phone, but Ron put his hand up and shook his head.

"If we're going to take pictures, I want them to be outside, with the ocean behind us."

"Are you sure you're up to that?" I asked, surprised.

Ron nodded as he pulled his covers back and for the first time in days, and with more spunk than I had seen since I'd met him, stood up and walked out to the beach with his daughter, granddaughter, and great-granddaughter following closely behind.

CHAPTER

14

The next few days were filled with taking pictures, sharing memories, and enjoying the time we had together. Ron even made his famous spaghetti and meatballs for dinner, which we all enjoyed. He was filled with more life than he had been when I first met him. Freddy and I even agreed to bunk together in the same room, so Annie, Angela and baby Kaitlyn could share the other room. It was cramped, but it seemed to work. We all wanted as much time with Ron as we could possibly have. After all, he was truly an amazing man. But Annie had questions about her mother, too.

"What was she like?" She asked.

"She was amazing." Ron answered. "And she's still here with us."

Annie looked confused. "I'm sure she's with us in spirit, dad."

He smiled, looking right toward where Estelles spirit was standing. "No, she's really here. Ask Samantha. She'll explain."

Annie and Angela looked at me curiously.

"Is he alright?' Annie asked. "Is he starting to hallucinate?"

I took a deep breath. "No, he's telling the truth. I don't know how you feel about this sort of thing, but I'm a medium. I can speak to deceased people. And your mother is sitting beside your dad. She's waiting for him to pass so she can follow him. She wants you to know she loves you all very much."

Annie looked at Angela, and back at me. "Is this some sort of joke?"

I shook my head. "No. Your mom is sitting right over there. Is there something you want to say to her?"

Annie was silent for a moment, thinking about what to say. Then she threw her head back and laughed.

"Mom, if you really are here with us, You do know those pancakes looked like a rabbit, right?"

Estelle laughed harder than I had ever seen her laugh.

"Yes, they were a poor excuse for Mickey Mouse. I'm sorry dear. I tried. I really did."

I repeated what Estelle said and Annie laughed. "That sounds exactly like my mom." She said. And that was one of those moments I thanked God I had a special gift. One tat could help a lot of people. And I didn't want to take it for granted anymore.

After a full day at the beach, everyone was exhausted, but Ron had one thing on his mind. "Samantha, In the hall closet is every birthday and Christmas present for Annie, from the time she disappeared until this past Christmas. I want her to open them now." He said.

I nodded and brought the gifts in one by one. Some, of course, were meant for a child. But Ron said those could be for baby Kaitlyn when she grew a little older. Angela was grateful and showed her baby the gifts. As the years progressed, the gifts were more like jewelry or ornaments. Annie was grateful for each and every one, giving her father a hug and thanking him. The last gift was a special one. It was a star he had bought, especially for Annie. And he had named the star 'Annies star.'

"This is amazing." She said, kissing her father on the cheek. "Thank you."

Ron smiled. "I have a telescope in the hall closet. Would you like to see your star?"

Annie nodded, enthusiastically. "I'd love to."

We all took turns gazing at Annies star that night before everyone went to bed. And I thought to myself the night couldn't be more perfect.

～∞～

I tossed and turned that night, unable to fall asleep. Probably because of all of the excitement of the day, and the fact that I had actually reunited a father and daughter after fifty years apart. That wasn't something you saw every day. And even if Ron Passed away in his sleep that night, Annie would always have these memories with her dad. That was really something special. After hours of tossing and turning, I tiptoed out to the front porch, sure that some fresh air would do the trick and send me off to dream land.

I sat there, listening to the sound of the waves crashing, feeling the cool breeze against my cheeks. I realized how much I was going to miss this place when I went back to Sacramento, back to my life before this summer, which seemed like it was so long ago. So much had happened in such a short amount of time. Then my thoughts turned to Charlie. And just as if he had read my mind, I saw him walking toward me from the beach. He was silent, but his eyes spoke a thousand words.

"Hi." Was all I could say.

"Hi." He said quietly.

I looked around to see if Mathew was nearby, but I didn't see him. "Where's Mathew?"

"He's spending the weekend with his grandmother." He answered. "Actually, both of his grandmothers. My mom and Grace's mom still spend a lot of time together. They're very close."

"That's good." I said. "I mean, for Mathew."

That was when I saw the yellow sundress, Grace's spirit was standing right behind Charlie.

"Tell him." she urged.

"I can't." I whispered.

"You can't what?" Charlie asked, confused.

I took a deep breath. "I can't leave things bad or awkward between us." I said. "It just doesn't feel right."

Charlie let out a sigh of relief. "Good, because it's been driving me crazy."

He followed me to a bench on the front porch, where we both sat. My heart was pounding as I thought about what to say next.

"I want to tell you I found Ron's daughter. And his granddaughter and great-granddaughter. I posted an ad on Facebook, and she replied. She was taken by a family who desperately wanted a child. I reunited them and it was wonderful, but also an emotional roller coaster. This has been an emotional week. So, I want you to know I haven't been ignoring you. I've just been busy. I've been thinking about you all the time though. I haven't stopped thinking about you. And I probably never will."

"I probably never will, either." he said, his voice full of certainty. "I think about you every minute, every day. I think about what an amazing woman you are, and there are so many things I like about you. Your confidence, how you always put others first. Finding Ron's Family is just one example. And I just want the chance to get to know you more, because I think I'm falling in love with you."

With those words, his lips pressed against mine, and again, it was a passionate kiss that I never wanted to end. I kissed him back; with all the passion I had in me. My heart pounded and my pulse raced. But I realized this couldn't be real until he knew the truth about me. I pulled away from him, and again, he looked confused.

"What's wrong Samantha? Please tell me. Did I do something wrong?"

I wanted to tell him everything, but at the same time, I wanted to enjoy this moment with him, untarnished by the truth.

"You know I have loved every minute with you and Mathew, right?" I said.

He nodded. "Yes, and that's why I'm so confused."

I smiled. "I still remember when I found Mathew on the beach. He seemed so small and afraid. And I could tell right away what a bright little boy he was. And then I met you, and I knew there was something special about you, too. Something I just couldn't get enough of."

Silence filled the air for a moment until Charlie found the words. "I was at a really low place that day. I never really told you this, but I even thought about taking my own life. I feel embarrassed to tell you this, but the reason Mathew wandered off that day was because I'd swallowed a bunch of sleeping pills, and he couldn't wake me up." Tears filled his eyes as he continued. "My little boy was so scared; he went to find help. And he found you."

I could feel the tears puddle up in my own eyes. "And I'm so glad he did."

Charlie took my hand in his, sending electrical currents all throughout my body. I wanted to kiss him, to tell him everything was going to be alright. That we could have a future together. But I knew there could be no future unless I told him the truth. Grace's spirit stood there, urging me to tell him.

"Alright." I said. "Here it goes. There is something about me that not that many people know, and when I tell people about this, they tend to run."

Charlie looked me straight in the eyes. "I can't imagine anyone running from you."

"I'm glad to hear you say that." I said squeezing his hand. "But they do."

"I would never do that." He assured me. "Whatever it is, you can tell me."

I took a deep breath, before I spat it out. "You know how you said you didn't believe in mediums?"

He nodded. "Yah, I've never really believed in that sort of thing."

"Well, what if I told you I am one?"

He narrowed his eyes, and suddenly they became cold. "What?"

"That's right." I said. "But I'm no phony. I'm the real deal. I was born with the ability to talk to the dead. My dad can do it too, so I guess I inherited this gift from him. Although, it isn't always a gift. I wish sometimes I was normal, just like everyone else. People treat me different when they find out what I can do."

Charlie scooted away from me, leaving a gap of distance. "I know you've been under a lot of stress lately, taking care of Ron and all, and that might make reality a little fuzzy."

I looked him straight in the eyes. "I've never been so clear. And guess who I have been talking to?"

His eyes narrowed, curious. "Who?"

"Grace." I said. "And she's standing right there." I motioned to where Grace was standing.

Charlie stood up now, slowly backing away. "You really are crazy."

I shook my head, feeling tears fall down my cheek. "I'm not crazy. She wants you and I to be together. She wants to know you and Mathew are happy before she can move on."

He backed up a few more feet. "I really think you should get some help, Samantha. You don't make any sense."

I looked down at the ground, realizing I wasn't going to win. Charlie was set in his ways, and nothing I said was going to change his mind.

"Ask him about our first date." Grace said. "It was at a sushi restaurant. It was Karaoke night, and he sang *'Sweet Caroline'*. He was so nervous, he spilled wine all over his favorite shirt. It was a Hawaiian shirt he lived in, blue with palm trees all over it, and he still tried to wear it until I finally got rid of it. Please, Samantha, make him believe this is real."

I told Charlie what Grace had said, but he seemed unphased.

"I have to go." He replied.

And just like every other guy I had dated before him, he walked, almost ran away, leaving me standing there cold and alone once again.

CHAPTER

15

I finally fell into a fitful sleep around 2am, thoughts of Charlie racing through my mind. I had hoped against hope that he would react differently, embrace my abilities with open arms, and that we would run into the sunset together, and live happily ever after. But that was all a dream.

I was awakened a little before 8am by the sound of Annie screaming. "Samantha! Come quick!"

I raced into Rons room, where I found Annie sitting by Ron on the floor. I knew right away that something wasn't right.

"I found him like this." She said, sadly. "I think he fell out of bed, and he won't wake up. I can't find a Pulse."

My heart sank in my chest as I kneeled down next to Ron, and took his arm in mine, trying to find a pulse. "I can't find one, either." I said, and we both started crying. Just seconds later, Freddy raced into the room, followed by Angela, who was holding baby Kaitlyn.

"What's wrong?" Freddy Asked, but as soon as he saw Ron laying like that, he knew.

"He's gone, Freddy." I said, confirming what we already knew.

Angela knelt down beside her mother, holding baby Kaitlyn close to her chest. Annie put her arm around her daughter, and they sobbed quietly. Freddy also knelt down beside me, tears were filling his eyes. I put my arm around him and wrapped him in a hug.

"It's going to be alright." I assured them. "This isn't the end. It's only the beginning."

And just then, the most beautiful light filled the room, and the spirits of Ron and Estelle hovered over the bed. I could tell by their expression that Freddy, Annie, Angela, and even baby Kaitlyn could see them.

Ron wrapped Estelle in a warm embrace, and I could tell they were happy, at peace. Ron looked at me and smiled. "Thank you again, Samantha. Thank you for everything."

"I ditto that." Estelle said with a wink.

"Tell Freddy, the answer to his question is yes." Ron continued. "He'll know what I mean. And tell our girls we love them all."

Annie looked at Ron's spirit hovering over the bed. "I know daddy. And we love you, too. I promise, every time I look at my star, I will think of you."

If it was possible, Ron's smile grew even bigger. "And don't let Kaitlyn forget about me, either."

Angela looked down at her baby and beamed. "I won't, grandpa."

"Alright, it's time." Estelle said. "I don't think the man upstairs likes it when we're late."

Ron nodded, and took her hand in his, and they both floated away together, leaving a beautiful glow in their path. They turned around and waved to us before they disappeared for good. We all watched until we couldn't see them anymore, wiping tears from our eyes. But they weren't sad tears, they were tears of joy.

"Wow, that was amazing." Freddy said. "I could actually see and hear them."

"I know." I said. "Sometimes right before they cross over, people who believe in life after death can see the spirits, just like I can. Usually just for a few minutes, though. Long enough to say goodbye."

"Well, I am grateful we had this last week with my dad." Annie said. "It's meant more to me than I will ever be able to express. And it's all thanks to you, Samantha."

"Well, it's not all thanks to me." I told her. "Freddy was actually the one who suggested I reach out on Facebook."

Annie looked at Freddy with a grateful smile. "Thank you, Freddy."

Freddy shrugged. "Well, it was just common sense, really. I can't believe nobody thought of it before."

I elbowed him playfully in the ribs. "Alright, smarty-pants. Just take a compliment, heh?"

He nodded. "You're welcome. But shouldn't we be calling the funeral home or something? Standing here with a dead body is kind of creepy."

I nodded. "Ron left excellent instructions about what he would want us to do. There is a folder in his office that explains everything."

With that, we all said one last goodbye to Ron's body. Although we knew he wasn't really there, it still brought us comfort somehow. I was the last one to leave the room, and before I shut the door, I looked back at him one last time. "Until we meet again." I said quietly, and clicked the door shut behind me.

The next few days were a blur, going through Ron's belongings and making sure he made it to his final resting place, which was of course right next to Estelle. He had left instructions for everything, including the funeral home he wanted to use, where he wanted his body laid to rest, and who he wanted to have his most precious possessions. Now that Annie had come back into his life, of course he wanted everything to go to her and her daughter.

'I want the beach house to be a place for family and friends to gather.' He said in his living trust. *'I hope that Annie, Angela and little Kaitlyn enjoy the house, and I would like Samantha and Freddy to visit, too. The more the merrier, I always say.'*

I was happy that he had included us, and I did think of Annie and Angela as lifelong friends. I pictured us sitting on the front porch for years to come, sharing memories of Ron and Estelle. And that thought made my heart glow with joy.

We visited Ron's grave before we all headed home. He had a beautiful headstone with granite, similar to Estelles. Engraved under his name it said, *'Loving husband, Father, Grandfather, and Great Grandfather.'* I was amazed and pleased that they were able to make the changes in such a short amount of time.

After we stopped by the beach house to make sure we hadn't forgotten anything, we all hugged and said our goodbyes.

"Thank you again for bringing us together again." Annie said, with tears in her eyes. "This really has been the best summer of my life."

I nodded. "It has been a summer we'll always remember. And I hope we can all make new memories at this house."

We all looked back at the house one last time. When I first arrived, I saw a broken-down dilapidated house with no hope. But now, when I looked at it, I saw nothing but hope. Hope for a bright future where many generations would gather. Where little Kaitlyn would run on the beach and make sandcastles. Where birthdays would be celebrated, and maybe even a wedding someday.

I wrapped my arm around my brother, feeling proud that he had contributed in more ways than I could count. He was growing up to be the kind of young man I always knew he could be.

"Are you ready to head home, little brother?" I asked.

He shrugged. "I guess."

I laughed. "I thought you would be dying to get home."

"I thought so, too." He said. "But a lot has happened in a month. In some ways it seems like we've been gone way longer, but in some ways, it feels like it flew by. Does that make any sense?"

I nodded. "It makes perfect sense. That's the strange time warp you're in when you grow up."

After we all said our final goodbyes and made plans to come down on a weekend the following month, we got in our cars and backed out of the driveway, going our separate ways.

"Aren't you going to say goodbye to that guy, Charlie?" Freddy asked. "I mean, you really seemed to like him."

I sighed. "I do. But it's complicated."

"How's it complicated?" He asked. "He likes you, and you like him."

I stopped at a red light, thinking about what to say next.

"That's true. But let's just say Charlie isn't a big fan of mediums, like me."

"Really, did he tell you that?" Freddy said with genuine concern in his voice.

I nodded. "He said were all phony's that are out for the money. And nothing could be further from the truth. I use my gift to help people."

Freddy nodded. "I know you do. And I want you to know I'm sorry for acting like a jerk. I used to be jealous of your ghost whisperer thing, but now I see it's more than just talking to dead people. I don't think I would want to be a medium. If I learned anything this summer, it's that I can be happy just being me."

I smiled, feeling pride wash over my body. "Little brother, that is exactly what you should be."

We both sat in silence as I drove along, listening to the classic rock station. When the song *Hey Jude* came on, I thought of Ron and Estelle, dancing at their wedding.

"Hey Freddy, I never asked what you asked Ron before he died. He told me the answer was yes."

Freddy took a deep breath. "Well, there's this girl I like. Her name is Hannah and she's really cool. I've liked her since we were in middle school, but I've always been afraid to ask her out. Like, what if she says no. So, I asked Ron if I should just do it. Take a chance and ask her out."

I beamed. "And he said yes."

Freddy nodded. "Just don't go getting all mushy on me, alright?"

I giggled. "I can't help it. My little brother is growing up."

He nodded. "It's not a big deal. She'll probably say no anyway."
"Freddy's got a girlfriend; Freddy's got a girlfriend." I chanted.
Freddy elbowed me from the passenger side. "Just keep driving, heh?"
So, I put my foot on the gas and continued on the long drive home.
Back to the life I had before the Summer that I will never forget.

CHAPTER

16

When I walked through the door to my house, it felt unfamiliar somehow, like I had been away for an eternity. I had asked a neighbor to bring in the mail for me, and a huge pile sat waiting on the entryway table. But that could wait. All I wanted to do was sit back on the couch and catch up on a Netflix series, or maybe a lifetime movie. Freddy felt the same because he went right to the guest room. We had a little time to kill before our parents came over for dinner. They were bringing takeout from our favorite Chinese restaurant, Blue Sky. I was looking forward to seeing them, and I was sure they felt the same way. We had a lot to share that was best done in person.

After scrolling through the shows available on Netflix, I decided to watch the last few episodes of Cobra Kai. I made a glass of iced tea and grabbed a snack of chips and Salsa before I sat down on my couch and put my feet up. A few minutes later, Freddy came and sat next to me.

"That's a good show." He said.

I nodded in agreement. "I loved the Karate Kid movies, so I was really excited to see these guys back on the screen. You want to watch? I have chips and salsa."

He grabbed a chip from the bowl and dunked it in the salsa. "Is this mild salsa?"

I nodded. "You know I can't stand spicy things."

"Wimp." He said with a chuckle. "My friends dared me to eat a ghost pepper once, and I ate it in one bite, without any water."

"Good for you." I praised.

He sat back on the couch, silent for a moment as we watched the show. "I really miss Ron."

"Me, too."

"But I'm glad I got to know him. "I wouldn't give up that time for anything."

"Me neither." I agreed.

"So, do you really think we'll get to see him someday?"

"I know we will." I said with a smile.

Freddy put his head on my shoulder, the same way he did when he was a little boy, and we watched the rest of the show in a relaxed silence.

As the second episode of Cobra Kai ended, there was a knock at the door. Perfect timing. I walked to the door and opened it. My dad stood there holding a bag of Chinese takeout, and my mom held a cake in one hand, and a bottle of wine in the other.

"Hi, mom. Hi dad." I said, giving each of them a hug. They seemed more relaxed somehow, and I noticed mom was wearing a new perfume. "You can put the food over there, on the table."

"As much as I loved Paris, I couldn't wait to get back to see you both." Mom said as she brought in her items and sat them on the table. Dad followed behind her and did the same. She looked over at Freddy and smiled. "I can't wait to hear all about your summer. I heard you went to Santa Cruz. You used to love the boardwalk when you were younger."

"Yah, it was pretty cool." Freddy said. "But it wasn't the best part."

"What was the best part then?" Mom asked, curious.

Freddy and I looked at each other. "It's a long story." We said in unison.

"Well, we have all the time in the world now." Mom said with a chuckle, "But right now I think we should eat while the food is hot."

We all made a plate and sat together, eating quietly for a while, enjoying the delicious food. Finally, my dad broke the silence.

"Your mom and I had an amazing trip. Samantha, I want to thank you for taking Freddy. I hope he was on his best behavior." He gave Freddy his best warning stare, and Freddy looked at me for defense.

"Actually, he was great." I said. "This was just the sibling bonding trip we needed."

Dad looked surprised. "Really? Well, I'm glad to hear that."

I nodded. "Well, I wasn't sure how it was going to go at first. I rented this beach house, and it looked great in the ad. But then we got there, and it was falling apart. The pool wasn't usable, everything was in disrepair, it was just a hot mess. And the man who owned the place, his name was Ron, and he was living there. So, I was pretty sure I was going to turn around and go home."

"Why didn't you?" mom asked. "It sounds dreadful."

"Because I wanted to stay." Freddy answered. "There was something about Ron, I could just tell he needed someone."

I nodded. "And he was right. He started telling us his whole life story, all about how he met his late wife, Estelle when they were kids, and how they went through a lot, but they were married over 57 years, isn't that insane?"

"Wow, and I thought seventeen years was a long time." Mom Said, reaching over to take dad's hand. I felt a pang of loneliness, wondering if I would ever find my soulmate.

"They were an amazing couple." I continued as we all took a few more bites of our food. "And I actually had the chance to talk to Estelle. She told me that Ron had stage 4 cancer. He was refusing treatment, and he had come to their house in Santa Cruz to die."

My parents looked at me, dumbfounded. "Wow, that's heavy." My mom said. "What did you do?"

"We stayed with him until the end." I said. "Freddy helped him fix up the house. Aunt Michelle and the twins even came out to visit."

My mom smiled. "She mentioned that she came to see you guys. She said she had a great time. But did you say Freddy helped to fix up the house?"

I nodded. "Yes, he did. And he did a great job, too."

Freddy beamed. "Well, I didn't do all the work. Ron helped too."

"I'm proud of you son." Dad said. "It sounds like you've really grown up over the summer."

Freddy nodded in agreement. "I think I have too, dad."

Dad took a sip of his wine before he looked at me with a serious expression. "Were you able to help Ron connect with Estelle?"

I nodded. "It was so beautiful, dad. And Ron was pretty open to the whole medium thing, after the shock factor, of course. She just wanted to know that Ron wasn't going to die alone."

"That sounds like a lot of pressure for the two of you." My mom said with concern in her voice.

"It was at first." I said, taking a sip of my own wine. "But it was worth it. I haven't even got to the best part."

"I don't know what could be better than helping a dying man connect with his wife." Dad said, matter of fact.

"Helping a dying man connect with the daughter he lost over 50 years ago, along with her daughter, and granddaughter."

Mom and dad's eyes both widened. "What?"

"Well, not to brag." Freddy said. "But I was the one who suggested the Facebook ad."

"Yes, you did, little brother." I said. "And it was amazing to watch him spend his last week with them. And Estelle was there too, of course. They made so many memories in that one week."

Dad cleared his throat and took a drink of his water. I could tell they were still processing what I was saying.

"Well, we were going to tell you all about Paris, but it sounds like that would be boring compared to the summer the two of you had." He said. "And Freddy, your mother and I have been doing a lot of thinking, and if you really want to change your name......."

Freddy held up his hand to cut him off. "I've decided I like my name. It's a good name, a strong name, and I'm proud to have it."

My mom looked like she was going to cry happy tears. She got up and wrapped her arms around Freddy.

"You really are growing up."

"Just don't go getting all mushy on me, ok?" Freddy said. "And you have 5 more seconds to hug me, so make it count."

She squeezed my brother tighter and looked over his shoulder toward me.

"Thank you, Samantha." She whispered.

"You're welcome." I whispered back.

Later that night, while Freddy and mom were playing an intense round of Battleship, dad and I sat out on my front porch, looking out at the street ahead. I suddenly longed for the ocean breeze and the sound of the waves. It was so calming compared to the sound of cars whizzing by.

"So, I'm curious about the young man you met while you were in Santa Cruz." Dad said. "What was his name again?"

I felt a fresh wave of tears brewing in my eyes. "Charlie."

"I take it things didn't work out?"

I shook my head. "No, they didn't. It turns out he is really against mediums. He thinks they are all phonies. And he doesn't believe in heaven, either. He's just like every other guy I have ever dated. And I'm done, dad. I don't want to try anymore."

I wiped a tear from my eye, and my dad looked at me sympathetically.

"If it's meant to be, he'll come around."

I sighed. "I doubt it. He seemed pretty sure that this is not something he wants to be part of."

"Well, your mother didn't want anything to do with me when I told her I was a medium. She thought I was crazy, told me to leave her alone. Said she wished she had never met me. But I gave her some space and time, and eventually, she accepted me for who I am."

"That's great, but just because it worked out for you and mom, doesn't mean it will work out for me. The world doesn't work that way, dad."

My tears started coming faster now, and my dad wrapped his arms around me. "Oh Samantha, I would give anything to take the hurt away for you."

"Well, you can't." I answered. "This is something I have to go through on my own."

He nodded. "I know, but to me, you'll always be my little girl. I want to fix things, make it easier. And I always feel guilty because I gave you this gift. It makes life more complicated. And people on the outside can't understand."

I shook my head. "Don't be sorry. I think about all the people I help, and it's so worth it. I don't want to change; I just want the rest of the world to change the way they think. To be more open. To believe in things even if they can't see them."

"I want that, too." he said, squeezing me tight.

And in that moment, all my sadness seemed to disappear.

CHAPTER

17

When the Bell rang on the first day of school at Crocker elementary, I was more than ready to greet my new students. I had spent countless hours preparing my lesson plan and getting my classroom ready, which was decorated with pastel rainbows and gnomes, two of my favorite things. Freddy had even come to help me get the classroom ready, reaching things on the high shelves that were out of my reach. He really had sprouted over the summer, in more ways than one. He got his learners permit, so I had taken him out for driving lessons a few times, and he was actually a pretty good driver. And he asked me to chaperone his first date with Hannah. Turns out she had always had a crush on him, too.

As my students filed into the classroom, I greeted them one by one, excited to start a new school year. I knew that would change by October, when I would be anxiously awaiting the Thanksgiving break. Teaching could be a draining profession, but the rewards were priceless. One little girl, with beautiful red hair that reminded me of Annie's came in clinging to her mother's leg.

"She has a little separation anxiety." Her mother explained.

I knelt down so I would be at her level. "My name is Miss Goodwin, and I'll be your first-grade teacher. What's your name?"

"Peyton." She said in a quiet voice.

"That's a nice name I said. And It's normal to be nervous on your first day of school, but I promise first grade is going to be so much fun. And I know it's a longer day than kindergarten, but your mom will be back before you know it. And we have a new art teacher this year, and I heard she has some fun things planned."

Peyton's eyes widened, and a bright smile spread across her face. "I love art!"

"She's supposed to come by later today." I said. "And I also have some fun field trips planned. Our first field trip will be to the pumpkin farm, and you will get to pick out your own pumpkin. How does that sound?"

"Great!" The little girl squealed with delight.

"Well, we're about to start class." I told her. "So, if you can hang your backpack on the hook over there and find your seat, we'll start with our good morning song and take roll."

Peyton gave her mother a hug and kiss, and went to hang her backpack up, and Peytons mother gave me a grateful smile as she waved goodbye and walked away.

Just as soon as I had everyone settled in, The Principal, Mr. Hubert walked in, holding a file in his hand. Suddenly, panic filled my body. Had another parent complained about my teaching? Was he here to fire me?

"Hello, Miss. Goodwin. I hope you had a nice summer." He said, with an expression that was hard to read.

"I did, thank you." I said looking at the file he held in his hand.

"I have a new student to add to your roster." he said, handing me the file. "This ones a little cutie, too. I think he will be a good addition to your class. His dad requested, actually, insisted, that he was in your class. He said he knows you."

I looked at the name on the file, and suddenly my heart stopped. *Mathew Bowen.*

As if on cue, Mathew ran into the classroom and tackled me with a hug, looking as cute as ever in his polo shirt and khaki pants, but even more grown up than the last time I had seen him. "Samantha!" He said. "How come you never said goodbye? I thought we were friends."

I knelt down to his level, feeling tears well up in my eyes again. "We are friends. It's just complicated. Grown up stuff."

He wrinkled his nose. "Well, you and my dad should just talk then. That's what you do when you have a problem. My kindergarten teacher taught me that."

"I wish it was that simple." I said

"His dad did want to speak to you." Mr. Hubert continued. "He's waiting in my office. I can take over your class for a bit while you go talk to him."

My heart drummed in my chest. What could we possibly say after our last conversation? But there was only one way to find out.

"Alright, Class, I need to take care of some important business. I will be back soon, but Mr. Hubert is in charge while I'm gone. Please show him your best behavior." I turned to Mathew. "You can have the seat over there, next to Peyton."

He hugged me one more time before he went to his seat, smiling from ear to ear. And he gave me the thumbs up sign as I walked out of the classroom.

As I walked toward the office, my throat felt tight, and my stomach was in knots. There was a time I wanted nothing more than to be close to Charlie. To feel his lips against mine, and the electricity that pulsed through my body when he touched me. But now I didn't know what to say. I knocked softly on the door to Mr. Huberts office before I walked in. Charlie sat in a chair behind the desk, his expression was blank.

"Hi, Charlie." I said.

He looked me in the eyes, and his expression seemed to soften a bit. "Hi, Samantha."

"It looks like Mathew will be in my class this year." I continued, trying to keep the conversation flowing.

He nodded. "I wanted him to have the best first grade teacher, and that is you. No other teacher can keep up with him and challenge him, and I know you will do that."

I smiled. "So, you moved here to Sacramento because you wanted Mathew to be in my class? There are plenty of other elementary schools, and plenty of great teachers out there."

He shook his head. "But they aren't you. I didn't just move here because of Mathew. I moved here to be closer to you."

I took a deep breath, thinking about how to respond. "I'm still a medium. I can't change who I am. And since you don't believe in that sort of thing, I don't see how it can work out between us. I deserve better than that, Charlie. I deserve someone who accepts me and loves me for who I am."

He paused for a moment; the silence was deafening. "Maybe I didn't before. But I do, now."

I narrowed my eyes. I felt confused, but also curious. "What does that mean? You don't just completely change your beliefs in two weeks. You were pretty clear about how you felt about people like me."

"That was before." He said. "But something happened since the last time we saw each other. Something life changing."

I crossed my arms over my chest, ready to listen to whatever it was, but still not confident Charlie was someone I could trust.

"I felt pretty low that night, after we talked last. The thought of losing you forever was more than I could take. I really was falling for you. I never thought I would feel that way again, after Grace, but you proved me wrong. I could see the future with you. And it was beautiful."

I nodded. "I was falling for you, too, Charlie. I saw that same future. But sometimes that's not enough."

He held up his hand. "Please let me finish. I started drinking, first wine, and then shots of tequila. I wanted to numb myself so I wouldn't have to hurt anymore. Mathew was with my mom, so I didn't have anything to distract me. So, I continued to drink, and I washed down a bunch of sleeping pills with vodka. I'm not even sure how many I took."

My heart sank. The thought of him being in such a low place was hard to take. But I listened as he continued his story.

"When my mom brought Mathew back the next morning, I passed out on the couch, and she couldn't wake me up. I wasn't breathing, I barely had a pulse. She started doing C.P.R on me, and Mathew actually called 911. He must have been so scared, but he knew what to do. He put the phone on speaker, so the operator could talk to my mom and keep them both calm until the paramedics arrived. On the way to the hospital, my heart stopped, everything stopped. I was technically dead."

My throat tightened as his words sunk in. "Did you see it?"

He nodded, knowing exactly what I meant. "I did. I saw heaven. It was so beautiful. There was grass, and the most beautiful, vivid colors I had ever seen. I saw my grandmother, and my uncle. They died years ago. I mean, they didn't look like them, but somehow, I knew who they were. And I felt so peaceful. More at peace than I ever had. I floated around, taking it all in. I never wanted to leave. I wanted to stay forever. But someone told me I couldn't stay. It wasn't my time."

"God." I whispered.

He nodded. "And all of a sudden, I was floating, looking down at my body. I didn't look like myself. I was swollen and I had a bunch of tubes and wires attached to me. The doctors were still trying to work on me, but they didn't look hopeful. And then, I floated over to where Mathew and my mom were sitting in the waiting room. Both of them were crying. And I knew as much as I wanted to go back to that beautiful place, there were people who needed me here. And then, I saw her. I saw Grace. She told me what I already knew. That our son needed his father. She also said you were telling the truth. She had been talking to you. And she wanted you to be part of Mathew's life. So, I went back to my body. Back to this life. And it took a while to recover, but here I am." Tears filled both of our eyes as he spoke. And all of a sudden, I saw Grace on the other side of the room. She seemed more at peace than she had before, an aura of calmness surrounded her. Charlie saw me looking in her direction. "Is she here, now?"

I nodded. "She is. And I think she's ready to cross over."

Charlies' eyes widened as he looked in her direction, and I could tell he could see her. "Goodbye my love." He said, tears falling down his cheek. "See you on the other side."

Grace waved, and blew a kiss in his direction, then she looked at me. "Take good care of them, Samantha."

My heart drummed even faster as I tried to comprehend what was happening. It felt like a dream, only it wasn't. It was real.

"I promise, I will." I whispered in a hoarse voice.

And with that, she waved one more time, and the most beautiful light glowed as she floated up, toward the sky. Charlie and I both watched until we could no longer see her. Then we looked at each other and smiled.

"I just want you to know how sorry I am that I didn't believe you before." Charlie said, his voice cracking. "But I believe you now. I will never doubt you again. And all I am asking for is a chance. And I know I probably don't deserve it; I don't deserve someone as wonderful as you. But I will spend the rest of my life proving to you that we were meant to be."

He looked at me, waiting for an answer. But I wasn't sure I was ready to give him one. After all, he had really hurt me. Was I really ready to dive into a relationship with someone who once thought I was crazy? I had already accepted that I was better off on my own. That I didn't need anyone to make me happy. And maybe I didn't. But I knew deep in my heart that I *wanted* Charlie and Mathew to be a part of my life. I couldn't deny that.

"You really broke my heart." I said.

He nodded. "I know. I was wrong. And if you tell me to leave, and never contact you again, I'll understand."

I smiled. "That's going to be a little difficult, with Mathew in my class. Unless you want to transfer him to a different school."

Charlie grinned. "I wouldn't dream of it. Mathew is exactly where he belongs."

"Well then, I guess I will see you after school. The bell rings at 3pm sharp. Don't be late. One of my biggest pet peeves is late parents."

"I won't be late." He promised.

"And there is a lot of paperwork you will need to fill out. I'm always looking for parent volunteers."

He nodded. "I would love that."

"Alright, well I should probably get back to my class." I said. " I'm sure Mr. Hubert is wondering where I am."

I turned and walked toward the door, but Charlie reached for my hand, and pulled me toward him, sending electrical currents to every inch of my body.

"What are you doing after school?" he whispered, his lips just inches from mine.

"I don't have any plans." I said with a grin. "Why do you ask?"

"Because Mathew and I have a tradition of going out for ice cream on the first day of school. And I'm sure he wouldn't mind if you joined us."

I paused for a moment, wanting to keep him on his toes. "I'd love to."

Charlie beamed and pressed his lips against mine, sending the same electrical currents through my body as he always did. And even though there was no white horse, and he was far from a knight in shining armor, no other moment in my life was more perfect than that moment. Well, at least up until then. There were hundreds of more even better moments ahead. I had never been more excited to see what the future had in store for me. And the future had never looked brighter.

ONE YEAR LATER

The little beach house in Santa Cruz became a gathering place, just as Ron and Estelle would have wanted. Annie brought her family often and she always made sure to invite us, too. It was amazing to see how much baby Kaitlyn had grown in the past year. Now, she toddled across the sand while her mother tried to keep up with her. Annie laughed, claiming she was just as active as Angela had been at that age. I thought to myself that Ron and Estelle would have both been beaming with pride.

Freddy walked along the beach, holding Hannah's hand. They had officially been dating for a year now, which must have been some kind of record in high school. The bachelor for life was no longer a bachelor, but he seemed happy. He'd even started eating meat again because Hannah happened to love meat. The things you'll do for love.

My aunt Michelle and the twins loved to come out to visit, too. Miles and Millie ran along the beach, collecting rocks and shells while Mathew gave them an in-depth lesson on each rock. They seemed interested in learning about the rocks, and I think my aunt Michelle was grateful that their attention was on something for more than two seconds.

Mathew had grown leaps and bounds during the past school year, both physically and academically. Although he was one of the youngest in my class, he was more than ready for second grade. I had already requested for him to be placed in Mrs. Violet's class, which was an advanced placement second grade class. I knew she would challenge him so he could continue to be the best that he could be. His mother would have been so proud. But now, that role went to me. And watching him grow up was a gift I would never take for granted.

My parents also loved spending time here. They walked along holding hands as the waves crashed against their ankles, huge smiles on each of their faces. As always, they were an example of what love should be. It was because of them that I was able to find my own version of happily-ever-after.

As for Charlie and me, we tried to take things slow at first, but that didn't last long. After a few months of dating, I moved in with him. Six months after that, we were married. It was a small ceremony on the beach with the most important people in our lives present, watching us say our vows. It was a magical day, one that I will never forget. Our song was 'I love you just the way you are' by Billy Joel, which was the perfect song for us.

Charlie volunteered every week in my classroom, and he found his own passion. He was offered a part-time job as a music teacher at Crocker elementary. I had no doubt that this was the perfect job for him.

Charlie came up behind me, wrapping his arms around me. He rubbed his hand over my stomach.

"How's our little one doing in there?"

I rubbed my hands over my stomach, in awe of the little life that was growing inside of me.

"I think she's doing just fine."

I felt a small kick that confirmed what I had said. Charlie moved his hand and smiled. This was the first time he had felt our baby kick.

"Did you feel that?" he asked, excitement in his voice.

I nodded. "I don't think she liked the Asian food I ate for lunch. This is her way of filing a complaint."

We both laughed, and we stood there in silence, watching the kids play on the beach. A year ago, I never would have guessed my life would turn out like this. As exciting as that was, one thought seemed to consume me. What if my unborn baby was like me? What if she was born with the gift to communicate with dead people? I knew first-hand how this gift made life more complicated. People weren't always kind to people who are different. Charlie seemed to read my mind.

"You know, I hope our daughter is exactly like you." He said so confidently I believed him.

"You do?" I whispered.

He nodded, kissing the back of my neck. "No matter what, she will be so loved. And she will have the best mother to guide her through whatever life brings her way."

I squeezed his hand, grateful again that I had a husband who always seemed to know how to make me feel better.

Mathew ran up to us, excitement in his voice. "Look, mom! I started a collection of rocks for the baby!" He held out a handful of colorful rocks. But that wasn't what caught my attention. That was the first time he had called me mom.

Charlie looked at me and smiled, feeling the emotion of that moment just as intensely as I did.

I bent down to his level. "They're beautiful. But you know I never want to take your mom's place."

He grinned. "I know. I will always remember her. But when she died, I was only four. I still called her mommy. I never grew up enough to call her mom. So that can be the name I call you if that's okay."

I pulled him into a hug and kissed the top of his head. "That's perfect."

Mathew took us each by the hand, and we walked into the sunset together, knowing that wherever life took us, we had each other. And that was more than enough.

www.ingramcontent.com/pod-product-compliance
Lightning Source LLC
LaVergne TN
LVHW041612070526
838199LV00052B/3104